UNFAIR ODDS

The hard cases turned to face him, then approached, remaining three abreast.

"You Clint Adams?" the lead man asked.

"That's right."

"We been asked to see you out of town."

"Is that a fact?"

"It is."

"I don't think so. I'm not ready to leave just yet."

Everybody in the saloon seemed to know what would happen next, because chairs scraped, tables overturned, and men hit the floor.

"You comin'?" the lead man asked.

"I said no," Clint said.

"Your funeral."

"You got that wrong . . . "

He switched his beer from his right hand to his left as the three men went for their guns. Almost regretfully he drew and killed the fastest of the three. The other two men still had not quite cleared leather when he shot them each once in the chest.

He holstered his gun and shifted his beer back to his right hand.

"*Your* funeral," he said, looking down at the lead man.

THE Gunsmith

164

THE OMAHA HEAT

J. R. ROBERTS

J

JOVE BOOKS, NEW YORK

THE OMAHA HEAT

A Jove Book / published by arrangement with
the author

PRINTING HISTORY
Jove edition / August 1995

ISBN: 0-515-11688-2

A JOVE BOOK®
Jove Books are published by The Berkley Publishing Group,
200 Madison Avenue, New York, New York 10016.
JOVE and the "J" design are trademarks
belonging to Jove Publications, Inc.

PRINTED IN THE UNITED STATES OF AMERICA

10 9 8 7 6 5 4 3 2 1

ONE

The telegram said there was no emergency—but where the hell was she?

Anne Archer's telegram to Clint Adams, sent from Lincoln, Nebraska, had asked him to meet her in Omaha. Clint had not seen Anne in a long time, nor had he seen her partners, Sandy Spillane and Katy Littlefeather. The three women were bounty hunters who had a very successful partnership. Clint didn't know if he was going to see all three in Omaha, or just Anne, but either way he was going to go to Omaha. Of the many women Clint had known in his life, Anne Archer was the one he'd choose to be with if somebody—some supreme being—told him he had to pick just one.

"This is a woman I've been looking forward to meeting for a long time," Rick Hartman said when Clint told him about the telegram.

1

"You'd have to leave Labyrinth to do that, Rick."

"Hey, I leave town . . . once in a while."

The last time he'd left town with Clint they had both ended up on a gambling train, only they ended up gambling with their lives.

"Come with me to Omaha, then."

"Can't," Rick said. "I need to hire two new girls. Besides, you really want me along when you see her again? I think not."

Clint looked down at the telegram in his hands.

"I wish she'd given me some idea why she wanted to meet me."

"Why worry? Maybe she got herself a big bounty and wants you to help her spend some of it. Maybe she just wants to see you again. Ever think of that?"

"In Omaha?"

"You ever been to Omaha?"

"No."

Hartman shrugged.

"You never know. Might be a lovely little city."

"Omaha," Clint said, shaking his head.

He left the next morning.

He rode into Omaha, very much looking forward to seeing Anne again. Her telegram had asked that he meet her at a hotel called the Nebraska Inn, and she told him what date she would be there by. He rode into town on that day and put Duke up at the nearest livery, leaving him in the care of an eighty-year-old hostler who had seven and a half fingers.

"Think you can handle him, old-timer?"

The man closed one eye and glared at Clint with the other.

"I been handlin' horses my whole life, sonny," he declared. He held up his hands—four fingers on one, three and a half on the other—and added, "How do ya think I got these?"

Satisfied, Clint then got himself a room at the inn and asked for Anne Archer.

"Who?"

"Anne Archer," he repeated. "She's a guest here. What room is she in?"

The clerk gave him a pinched look, peering at him from just above his pince-nez.

"Sir, I know all the guests in this establishment and there is no one by that name."

"She's got to be here," Clint said. "Check your book . . . please." Clint had not yet signed the book himself.

"I don't have to check my book, sir," the clerk said. "I know all—"

"She said she was gonna meet me here," Clint said. "Check the damn book!"

The man took an inadvertent step back and said, "Very well, sir, if you insist."

The clerk opened the book, scanned a page or two, and then said, "No, I'm sorry, she's not here."

"Let me see."

"Certainly. You, uh, have to sign in anyway."

Clint reversed the book so he could read it. There were quite a few registrations for this day and the day before, but Anne Archer's name was not among them.

"I don't understand," he said. "She asked me to meet her here."

"Perhaps she simply hasn't arrived yet, sir," the clerk said. "The, uh, day is still young."

"Yes," Clint said, nodding, "yes, maybe I'm worrying needlessly."

"Yes, sir," the man said. "Would you, uh, sign the book, please?"

"Huh? Oh, yeah, sure. . . ."

Clint signed his name, and the clerk turned the book around to read it.

"Clint . . . Adams?" he asked, giving each name a life of its own.

"That's right."

The clerk swallowed, realizing who it was he had been adopting an attitude with.

"We have several rooms available, sir," he said, eager to make amends. "Would you like one overlooking the street?"

"Is there a balcony of some kind?"

"No, sir."

"Then I'll take it."

Clint had long ago stopped taking rooms with balconies outside. He'd had too many people come in through the window and try to kill him.

"It's a fine room, sir. I'm sure you'll like it."

"I'm sure I will."

The clerk gave him the key and said, "Room eleven, sir."

"Thanks."

"Shall I have someone take your, uh, belongings up?"

Clint had his rifle and saddlebags with him.

"No, I can handle it."

"Yes, sure, of course you can."

Clint started away, then turned back.

"Is there something else I can do for you, sir?"

"Yes, you said you had several rooms available."

"That's right, sir."

"Could we hold one for my friend?"

"Uh, that would be the lady?"

"That's right."

"I don't see why not, sir. What was her name again?"

"Archer," Clint said, "Anne Archer."

"Ann—"

"With an *e*."

"Of course," the clerk said, making the addition, "with an *e*. There. We'll hold room five for her, sir. It's a nice room."

"Thanks."

"Will, uh, will you be paying for both rooms?"

"Does it matter who pays?" Clint asked. "They'll be paid for. Isn't that enough?"

"Oh, of course, sir," the clerk said, "I didn't mean to imply—"

"No implication taken," Clint said. "Do you have bath facilities?"

"Oh, yes, sir, we have many modern—"

"I just want a hot bath," Clint said. "Can you arrange that?"

"Yes, sir. It will be ready in fifteen minutes."

"Good," Clint said. "I'll be back."

The clerk watched nervously as Clint went up the steps, and when he was out of view the man let out a sigh of relief that, in his ignorance, he hadn't gotten himself killed.

TWO

Clint dropped his gear off in his room, took a clean shirt from his saddlebag, and went back downstairs for his bath. After the bath he checked with the desk clerk again, who shook his head. Anne Archer had not arrived yet.

It had been Clint's experience with Anne that she did what she said she was going to do. If she said she'd be in Omaha, Nebraska, on this date, at this hotel, she'd be there—if she could. By all rights he should give her until midnight before he started to worry, but the nature of her business—bounty hunting—made him worried already.

He spent the rest of the day sitting in the hotel lobby, waiting. His presence made the desk clerk so nervous that the man was constantly dropping things. At one point the man worked up the courage to ask Clint if he'd like to wait in the hotel's saloon.

"I will let you know as soon as your friend arrives," the man offered.

"No, thanks," Clint said. "I think I'll just wait right here."

Later, Clint guessed that the clerk must have sent for the sheriff. When the lawman walked into the lobby, though, Clint thought nothing of it. He watched as the man packing the star walked to the desk, spoke with the clerk briefly, and then came over to where he was sitting.

"Clint Adams?" the man asked.

"That's right."

Clint looked up at the sheriff, figured him to be in his early forties or thereabouts. He had the look and carriage of an experienced man.

"My name is Sheriff Luther Macy."

"Glad to meet you, Sheriff."

The man indicated the cushion next to Clint on the hotel lobby sofa and asked, "Mind if I sit?"

"Why would I mind?"

Macy sat.

"I understand you registered at the hotel this afternoon."

"That's right."

"You here on business?"

"What kind of business do you think I'd be here on, Sheriff?"

"You'd know that better than me."

Clint was worried about Anne Archer and annoyed that the sheriff had chosen this moment to interrogate him. Still, that didn't mean he had to give the lawman a difficult time.

"I'm not here on any sort of business, Sheriff," he said patiently. "I simply came here to meet with a friend."

"I see."

"My friend is a woman," Clint continued. "She was supposed to be here today, and she hasn't arrived yet. I'm a little worried."

"Well, you know women," Macy said. "They're never on time."

"This one is," Clint said, "always."

"She sounds reliable."

"She is."

"Makes her a rare woman, in my book," Macy said. "What's her line of business?"

Clint wondered if this was going to open some sort of can of worms, but he answered the question anyway.

"She's a bounty hunter."

"What?"

Clint nodded as the sheriff looked at him incredulously.

"A woman bounty hunter?"

"She has two partners," Clint said, "and they're women, too."

The sheriff needed a moment to digest this.

"You haven't taken up bounty hunting, have you, Mr. Adams?" he asked then. "I mean, I haven't heard anything about you—"

"No, Sheriff, I haven't taken up bounty hunting. Like I said, I'm just here to meet a friend."

"Your friend," Macy asked, "is she comin' here on business?"

"Sheriff," Clint said, "I won't know that until she gets here."

"No," Macy said, "I guess not."

"There's no law against me waiting here, is there, Sheriff?" He was starting to realize that the clerk had somehow gotten the sheriff over here to talk to him.

Macy stood up and said, "No law that I know of, Mr. Adams. I hope your friend gets here soon."

"So do I, Sheriff."

Clint watched as the sheriff walked over to the desk to talk to the clerk again. He could tell by the look on the man's pinched face that he wasn't happy with what the lawman was telling him. The sheriff ended the conversation by shrugging his shoulders and walking out. The clerk looked over at Clint, then looked away hurriedly when he saw that Clint was watching him.

Clint decided to ignore the jumpy little man. If the clerk thought that he was going to suddenly draw his gun and start shooting up the place, that was his problem.

THREE

By ten p.m. Clint felt justified in being worried. He didn't feel he needed to give it until midnight.

He had started alternating between the hotel lobby and a chair out in front of the place. The clerk seemed to take this as a sign that he wasn't going to shoot up the hotel lobby and had relaxed some. At ten he was relieved by another man, and both clerks huddled with their heads together while clerk number one told clerk number two about Clint Adams.

Clint ignored the two of them and went outside at 10:05. He stared up at the moon and wondered what the hell his next move should be. He patted his shirt pocket and felt the piece of paper there. He took it out and stared at it. It was the original telegram from Anne, asking him to meet her here. It had been sent from a telegraph office in Lincoln, Nebraska.

He turned and went back inside. The new clerk

11

was now alone behind the desk. He was an open-faced man in his thirties who smiled as Clint came to the desk.

"You really had Earl scared all day," the man said. "What did you do to him?"

"Do you have to do something to Earl to scare him?" Clint asked.

"Not really. He scares pretty easily. What can I do for you, Mr. Adams?"

"What's your name?"

"Bob."

"Bob, does the hotel have a telegraph key?"

"No, sir, but there's an office down the street."

"It would be closed now, though, wouldn't it?"

"Yes, sir, it would."

Clint frowned. He'd have to wait until morning to send a message to Lincoln—asking what, of whom? He needed someone to look for Anne Archer there, and the likely person was the local sheriff. That meant that before going to the telegraph office in the morning he'd have to stop by Sheriff Macy's office and find out the name of the sheriff in Lincoln.

"Is there something else I can do?" Bob asked.

"No, I guess not. Not tonight. What time does the bar stay open till here in the hotel?"

"Still got a few hours yet."

Clint nodded and tucked Anne's telegram back into his pocket.

"I'll be in there," he said to the clerk.

"If the lady comes in, I'll tell her," Bob promised.

"Thanks," Clint said, but he doubted that Anne Archer would be arriving tonight.

Clint spent the next couple of hours sitting at a table, nursing two beers and rebuffing the advances of two girls who worked for the hotel. They took turns trying to get him interested in them, but Clint had too many women on his mind as it was.

He was worried about Anne, and he was wondering where her two partners, Sandy Spillane and Katy Littlefeather, were. Were they with her? Or were they also to meet her here? The women did not have a base of operations, as he did with Labyrinth, Texas, so there was really no way to track them down either. Still, he decided that when he sent a telegram to the sheriff of Lincoln the next morning he'd ask about all three women. Maybe he'd get lucky and find Sandy or Katy there.

He knew that all three women were extremely capable of taking care of themselves. If he knew they were all together he probably wouldn't have been so worried, but Anne's telegram had made no mention of her partners. That was what led him to believe that she would be meeting him alone. How far was Lincoln from Omaha anyway? What kind of trouble could she have run into in between?

"Another beer?"

Clint looked up and saw one of the women standing next to him, the horse-faced brunette. Actually that wasn't fair. Her face was a little long, but she wasn't at all unattractive—except when she smiled.

Too bad. Smiling improved most women's looks. This one was unfortunate enough to have it the other way around.

"No, thanks."

She put her hands on her slender hips and asked, "Change your mind about anything else?"

"I don't think so."

Even if he'd been in the mood for some female companionship, she wasn't his type. She had hardly any hips and breasts at all, and he had the feeling that if he went to bed with her he'd end up with a dozen or so bone bruises by morning.

She shrugged her bony shoulders and walked away. By now he thought the two women must have had a bet on which of them would get him into bed. The blonde had a better chance, since she was rather buxom, but neither of them had *much* of a chance— not with the frame of mind he was in.

Finally he decided to call it a night. There was no use sitting there going over and over it in his mind. In the morning, if Anne hadn't shown up yet, he'd follow through on his plan to send a telegram to Lincoln.

He pushed the remainder of the second mug of beer away, stood up and walked out into the lobby. The clerk, Bob, looked at him and sadly shook his head. Clint waved at the man, finding him much more palatable than the first clerk, and went to his room.

FOUR

Clint slept fitfully that night, dreaming of all sorts of calamities befalling Anne Archer during her ride from Lincoln to Omaha, Nebraska. He rose for good just before daylight and went downstairs to see if he could get some breakfast.

"You look awful," Bob said.

"Didn't sleep very well."

"This lady must mean a lot to you."

"She does."

"Well, I wish I could tell you she showed up, but . . ."

"That's okay," Clint said. "Can I get something to eat this early?"

Bob held up his hand.

"Let me go in and arrange it."

He was gone ten minutes and when he returned he told Clint to go into the dining room and sit down.

"They'll serve you."

"You seem to have some pull in this hotel," Clint observed.

"I should," Bob said. "My uncle owns it."

Clint nodded.

"That would do it. Thanks."

"Forget it," Bob said. "Enjoy your breakfast."

Clint waved a hand and went into the dining room. All of the tables still had chairs stacked on them except one, which he assumed had been cleared for him. He sat down and a waiter appeared, a small man in his fifties, with unusually large hands. Those hands probably came in handy when he had to balance a number of plates at one time.

"What's good?" Clint asked.

"Best steak and eggs in town," the man said, without hesitating.

"Good," Clint said, "bring it on."

The man was true to his word. Clint didn't know if it was the best steak and eggs in town, but it was the best he'd had in a while. The only drawback was that the coffee wasn't strong enough. He told the waiter that when the man asked how everything was.

"Next time you let me know you want it strong," the man said. "That's the way I drink it."

"I'll remember," Clint said. "Thanks."

He left the hotel with his appetite satisfied. Now he had to work on the rest of him.

It was still too early for the sheriff to be in his office, so Clint simply sat down on the edge of the boardwalk and waited for the man to arrive.

He spotted the sheriff walking across the street and stood up to greet him.

"I don't usually have people waiting for me to get here in the morning," the sheriff said, unlocking the office door. "Come on in."

Clint followed the man in and waited until he was sitting at his desk.

"Did your friend get here?"

"No."

"What can I do for you, then?"

"I need the name of the sheriff of Lincoln."

Macy frowned.

"What for?"

"That's where she was coming from."

"You think maybe something happened to her there?"

"I hope not," Clint said. "I don't know what to think. Getting in touch with someone there is the only thing I can think to do, and the sheriff seems the logical choice."

"Makes sense to me," Macy said. "His name is Ed Chadwick. Been sheriff there for almost as long as I have here."

"How long is that?"

Macy frowned.

"It's been *so* long I sometimes forget how long . . . but it's been twelve years for me. I think he got his job the year after I did."

"Can I use your name?"

"Sure," Macy said, "tell him I said he'd help you. I

don't know how much good it will do you, but go ahead."

"You and him don't get along?"

"Let's just say we ain't friends."

"Is he a good man?"

"Oh, he's a good lawman, all right," Macy said. "We've just had us some, uh, what you'd call jurisdictional disputes."

"I see."

"He'll do what he can for you, Mr. Adams," Macy said, "same as I would."

"I appreciate your help, Sheriff."

"If he can't help you, and she still hasn't gotten here by later today, I guess we could go out and look for her between here and Lincoln."

"I guess I could do that myself," Clint said, standing up, "if it comes to that."

"Let me know what happens, anyway, will you? I don't like mysteries, and I'd like to see this one solved."

"You and me both, Sheriff," Clint said, and left to go to the telegraph office.

FIVE

Clint had composed the telegram overnight, changed it over breakfast, and then again during the walk to the telegraph office. As he entered the office he thought he had it right, but in the middle of writing it down he changed it still again.

"Send it," he said to the clerk.

"Are you sure?" the man asked. Clint had scratched out much of what had been on the page.

"I'm sure," Clint said. "Send it."

The clerk turned the slip of paper over and squinted at it.

"I can't read it," he complained.

"How about if I dictate it?"

"Well . . . okay."

That turned out to be a bad idea. He tried to change the message halfway through, but the clerk

19

told him he couldn't because he'd already sent half
of it.

When it was finally done he paid the clerk, then
gave him a little extra.

"What's this for?"

"Come and find me when the reply comes."

"Where?"

"The hotel, or the saloon nearest to it."

"Well . . . okay."

Clint left the office, hoping that a reply would be
quick in coming.

He had addressed the telegram to Sheriff Ed Chadwick, asking for information on any of the three lady
bounty hunters: Anne Archer, Sandy Spillane, and
Katy Littlefeather.

"Littlefeather?" the clerk had asked.

"That's right."

"Spell it," the man said.

Clint did the best he could, never having seen the
name in print himself.

He signed his name and the name of the town, then
added the name of the hotel.

He walked back to the hotel and as he entered saw
that the first clerk he'd met yesterday was on duty
behind the desk. He walked past him to the dining
room, because the bar was not yet open.

The same waiter who'd served him breakfast met
him at the door.

"Still hungry?"

"I need coffee," Clint said, "strong coffee."

"Coming up, Mr. Adams. Just take a table."

It was between breakfast and lunch, so there were more empty tables than full ones.

"Can you find me a newspaper?" he asked the man before he could walk away.

"It would be a local paper," the waiter warned.

"That's okay," Clint said. "I just need something to read."

"I'll take care of it."

The waiter soon returned with a pot of strong coffee and a copy of the *Omaha Herald*.

"Thanks. What's your name?"

"Luke, sir," the man said. "Luke Hardy."

"What do your friends call you?"

"Hardy."

"Well, thanks for the paper, Hardy."

"Taste the coffee. That pot is just the way I like it, myself."

Clint poured out a cup and took a sip. It was scalding hot and strong enough to take the paint off the side of a barn.

"It's perfect," he said.

The waiter nodded with satisfaction and went off to serve someone else.

Clint spread the newspaper out on the table and poured his cup full. There didn't seem to be anything much happening locally. Apparently someone was breaking into businesses at night and stealing things—not money, but items that were of no real value to anyone. Clint thought it was probably just someone who enjoyed the act of breaking into someone else's home or store and stealing

something. Some people needed the damnedest
things in their lives to keep themselves occupied, if
not happy.

There was an article about someone trying to start
some baseball teams in Omaha. Clint had played
baseball very briefly in the East. The same talents
that made him a deadly shot with a gun had made
him a fine pitcher. He wondered if that game would
ever really become popular.

There were some obituaries, mostly elderly citi-
zens who had passed away in the night from some
illness or simply old age.

Clint wasn't really looking for anything in particular. He wanted to pass the time while waiting for
the reply from Lincoln, and this was simply a way
for him to do it.

He reached the last page of the paper just as Hardy
returned to his table.

"Found another newspaper," the man said. "It's a
couple of days old."

"That's fine."

"It's not local."

"That's not a problem either."

Hardy handed Clint a copy of a two-day-old
Lincoln Register.

SIX

Clint put aside the Omaha paper and opened the one from Lincoln. The front page screamed out at him with an item that dwarfed anything that was happening in Omaha.

MURDER! the headline proclaimed.

Apparently, murder in Lincoln, Nebraska, was unusual. The article was written by the paper's editor, who was outraged that this crime should occur in "our" town. He was especially concerned because the victim was a woman. She had been strangled, and then stabbed. Why, Clint wondered, if she had been strangled did she have to be stabbed as well? This was a question that was not asked or answered in the newspaper.

The article ended with the editor—a man named Jefferson Lakewood—demanding that the sheriff,

Ed Chadwick, do something about bringing the culprit to justice.

Clint scanned the remainder of the newspaper and then set it aside. What did the editor think the lawman was doing? Any sheriff worth his salt would want to solve a murder that happened in his city or town, and Sheriff Macy had said that Sheriff Chadwick was a good man.

What concerned Clint was that nowhere had the story mentioned who the dead girl was or what she looked like. It could have been Anne, for all he knew, or Sandy, or Katy. The only way to find out was to send another telegram to Sheriff Chadwick, even before he received the answer from the first one.

"Finished with the coffee?" Hardy asked. He had seen Clint stand up and had rushed over.

"Hardy, do you know anything about this?"

"What?" Hardy asked, taking the Lincoln newspaper from Clint. "Oh, this murder?"

"Yes."

Hardy shook his head.

"No, I don't. In fact, I didn't even read this article. Is it good?"

"It's interesting."

"What's it about?"

"A woman being killed."

Hardy's eyes widened.

"And you think you know her?"

"I don't know what to think," Clint said. "I was supposed to meet a woman, a friend of mine, here. She was coming from Lincoln."

"Christ, it could be her."

"It could be," Clint said. "I've got to find out for sure."

"How?"

"By sending a telegram to Lincoln. Thanks for the newspapers, Hardy. Can I keep this one?" He held up the Lincoln paper.

"Sure. I'm just sorry there was bad news."

"Maybe there was," Clint said, "and maybe there wasn't."

As Clint left the dining room Hardy called out, "Let me know what happens."

Clint waved and left.

SEVEN

"I was just about to come looking for you," the clerk said as Clint entered the telegraph office.

"My reply came in?"

The clerk nodded.

"Just now."

Clint put out his hand and the man handed him the answer. It was addressed to Clint and it had one line on it: IF YOU WANT ANSWERS, COME TO LINCOLN. It was signed: "Sheriff Ed Chadwick."

"Son of a bitch," Clint said.

"Not what you wanted, huh?"

Clint ignored the man.

"Want to send a reply to the reply?"

Clint's intention had been to send another telegram, but suddenly he knew that Sheriff Chadwick was right. The only way to find out what he wanted was to go to Lincoln.

26

"No," Clint said, "no reply."

He went out the door and headed for the sheriff's office.

Macy looked up as Clint entered the office.

"Who's chasing you?"

"Do you know anything about this?" Clint asked, thrusting the Lincoln newspaper at the man.

Looking puzzled, Macy took the newspaper, gazed at the front, and then nodded.

"You mean this murder?"

"Yes, the murder."

"What's this got to do with—oh, wait. A woman was murdered, right?"

"That's what it says."

"But it doesn't say who the woman was, right?"

"Right."

"So it could be your friend."

Clint scowled.

"Well, I hope it's not," Macy said, dropping the paper on his desk, "but to answer your question, no, I don't know much about it. My guess is Sheriff Chadwick doesn't either."

"What makes you say that?"

"He usually sends me a telegram when he's looking for somebody," Macy said. "He probably has no idea who committed this murder, because I'm not on the lookout for anyone."

"I see."

"Did you send him a telegram like you planned?"

"I did."

Clint handed Macy the reply. The man read it, shaking his head.

"Chadwick is kind of closemouthed," Macy said, handing it back. "It's one of the things that makes him difficult to like."

"I don't want to like him," Clint said, "I just want to talk to him."

"You want me to send him a telegram and see if he'll tell me anything?"

"No," Clint said, "I've decided to ride to Lincoln and talk to him myself. Meanwhile, I can keep a sharp eye between here and there."

"Sounds like a good plan."

"How far is Lincoln from here?"

"A good day's ride. I'd suggest you start out tomorrow morning. You should be there before dark."

"Thanks for the advice." Clint picked up the newspaper. "I'm sorry I came busting in here."

"That's okay," Macy said. "Just let me know if I can help you. My guess is you'll be coming back here. Am I right?"

"Yes, you are," Clint said. "This is where she said she'd meet me. I'll have to come back here . . . if I don't find something out in Lincoln."

The only thing that would keep Clint from returning to Omaha was if he found out that the dead girl was Anne Archer. If that was the case he wouldn't be leaving Lincoln until he found out who did it.

EIGHT

Clint returned to the hotel. It occurred to him that all he had seen of Omaha was the hotel, the sheriff's office, and the telegraph office. He wasn't in the mood to sightsee, though. He entered the lobby, then walked back out again. He decided to go to the livery to check on Duke, make sure the big, black gelding was ready for a day trip the next morning.

As Clint entered the livery, the old man with seven and a half fingers fronted him.

"Checking up on yer big gelding?"

"That's right."

"Don't think I'm takin' good care of him?"

Clint looked the oldster up and down and knew that if he answered in the affirmative the old man might challenge him.

"I'm sure you're taking great care of him," Clint

said. "I just wanted to tell you to have him ready to ride in the morning."

"When in the morning?"

"Early."

"First light?"

"If you're up that early."

The man spit a glob of tobacco juice halfway across the livery and said, "Hell, when you get to be my age you learn not to waste so much time sleepin'. I'll be up, and he'll be ready."

"Much obliged, old—uh, what's your name, anyway?"

"Real name's Chester," the man said, "but folks round here just call me 'Fingers.'" He cackled, held up his hands, and asked, "Kin ya guess why?"

Clint could guess.

"Mind if I have a look at him, since I'm here?"

"I don't mind none," Fingers said. "Fact is, he's been kinda mopey. I think he misses ya. He's in number six, at the back."

"Maybe he does miss me. Thanks, Fingers."

Fingers waved with the hand that had four digits and walked away. Clint walked back to number six and saw Duke standing straight and tall, as if he'd been waiting for him.

"Going for a ride tomorrow, big fella," he said, patting the big gelding's neck. "We've got to see if we can find out what's going on here."

Duke just shook his head and then pawed the ground some.

"I know you don't like standing around," Clint

said. "I'll be by nice and early to pick you up. Mean-while, Fingers'll take good care of you." He lifted the horse's head and looked him in the eye. "Don't be biting off any of his fingers, though. He doesn't have any to spare."

Duke gave him a baleful look.

"I knew you'd understand."

He gave Duke's neck one last pat, then turned and left the livery without seeing Fingers again.

From across the street a man followed at a dis-creet distance as Clint walked from the livery to the hotel and went inside. The man then found a door-way across the street and settled into it. His job was to keep an eye on Clint Adams and nothing more, and that suited him. He knew the reputation of the Gunsmith, and he wasn't being paid enough to do anything but watch.

"Mr. Adams?"

It was the clerk, the first one he'd met the day before.

"Yes?"

"Uh, your friend, she hasn't shown up yet."

Clint stared at the man. Was he actually trying to be helpful?

"I know it," Clint said, "but thanks anyway."

"Oh—well, I was just trying to be, uh—"

"You can help me, though."

"Oh? How?"

"I'll be leaving town tomorrow, but I'd like you to

hold that room. I shouldn't be gone more than a day or two."

"That won't be a problem, sir," the clerk said. "We'd be glad to hold your room for you."

"Thank you."

"Certainly, sir."

As Clint went up to his room he was at a loss what to do with himself. It was too late to start for Lincoln today. He'd only have to stop riding and camp before he got halfway there. What, then, should he do until it was time to turn in? Poker was out. He just didn't have the concentration. A woman? Not while he was worried about Anne Archer.

He decided to stay in his room until dinnertime and then take a walk and see some of Omaha before getting something to eat. He figured that by the time he was ready the desk clerk Bob should be on duty, and he could probably recommend a good restaurant to eat in.

After dinner he'd play it by ear. Maybe a couple of beers and then an early night so he could get that early start in the morning.

He took off his gun belt, kicked off his boots, reclined on the bed and promptly fell asleep.

NINE

Across the street the man waited an hour before deciding that he could risk leaving just long enough to report to the man whom he was working for. Adams didn't seem to know many people in town, and the chances were good that he'd still be in the hotel when he got back.

He was actually hoping that his boss would replace him. It made him real nervous to be following a man who had a reputation like the Gunsmith did.

"You did what?" the man behind the desk bellowed. "You left him where?"

"He's probably asleep in his room," the man said, in his own defense.

"When I tell you to keep an eye on somebody," his boss said, "that's what I expect you to do."

"Uh, I just thought—"

"You don't have to tell me what you thought, Castle," the other man said. "You're afraid of Clint Adams."

"Damn right I am . . . uh, sir."

"Well, I told you all you had to do was watch him. I've got somebody else coming in who will take care of the rest."

"The rest?"

The man behind the desk said, "Just get back to that hotel and don't let Clint Adams out of your sight. A man named Barlowe will be coming by soon."

"Henry Barlowe?"

"That's right," the other man said, "but don't call him Henry to his face. He prefers Hank. I only hired him to kill Adams, but I'm sure he'd be glad to throw you in for free."

Castle swallowed hard. Great. Now he had two men with reputations to be afraid of.

After Castle left, the man who hired him walked to his window and looked outside. Barlowe was supposed to arrive today from Council Bluffs, Iowa, where he lived. For a man with a big reputation, Henry "Hank" Barlowe sure picked a small place to settle down. These days he only left Council Bluffs for very special jobs—like killing a man of Clint Adams's stature—and since there weren't too many men like that around anymore, that meant he left very rarely.

Today, however, was one of those days.

Barlowe had a reputation. Oh, not one as far-reaching as Clint Adams's, but in facing Adams he had youth on his side, as he was at least a dozen years younger.

The man returned to his desk and sat down. Barlowe would not have agreed to the job if he didn't think he could handle Clint Adams. All the man had to do was sit back and wait.

TEN

When Clint awoke he was annoyed with himself for falling asleep. A quick look outside told him that he'd been asleep for a couple of hours. There was still a lot of daylight left, and time for a leisurely walk before dinner. It just bothered him that he'd drifted off so readily.

He pulled his boots back on, strapped on his holster, and went downstairs. As he had figured, Bob was working at the desk.

"Hello, Mr. Adams. What's been going on?"

He took the time to explain the day's happenings to the clerk because the young man was interested. It also helped pass some time.

"This sheriff from Lincoln doesn't sound very helpful, does he?" Bob asked.

"No, he doesn't," Clint said, "but maybe he'll tell me more in person."

"I hope so."

"Bob, I was thinking of taking a walk and I wondered if you could recommend someplace to have dinner?"

"There are a lot of good little restaurants and cafés, Mr. Adams. I don't know where you're gonna end up, so I'll write down a few names for you. You'll probably run into one of them."

Clint waited while Bob made a short list and handed it to him.

"Thanks very much."

"When will you be leavin' for Lincoln?"

"First thing in the morning."

"Think you'll be comin' back this way?"

"I hope so."

"I hope so, too. You're an interesting man to talk to."

"We'll talk some more, Bob," Clint said, shaking the young man's hand. "I promise."

"You do what you gotta do, Mr. Adams," Bob said. "We got plenty of time to talk."

Clint nodded and walked out of the hotel, tucking Bob's list into his shirt pocket.

Back at his post, Castle saw Clint Adams leave the hotel and fell into step with him. He stayed well back, though, and across the street. All he had to do was keep him in sight, and he'd be doing his job. He didn't have to get real close to do that.

Staying back this far suited him just fine.

•   •   •

At that moment Henry "Hank" Barlowe rode into town. He didn't usually like crossing the river from Iowa into Nebraska, but he figured this trip would be well worth it. For one thing, the man he worked for paid well. For another, since the target was Clint Adams, Barlowe had doubled his price and it had been agreed on.

Instead of leaving his horse at the livery, Barlowe rode down a side street and tied his horse off at a hitching post in front of a vacant building. With any luck he'd do the job and be gone before anyone knew what had really happened.

His information was that Adams was staying at the Nebraska Inn. His employer had a man named Castle keeping an eye on him. Castle had been described to him as a pasty-faced man in his thirties. Following Clint Adams would make the man even more pasty-faced than usual, Barlowe was sure.

He was wearing a .44 Colt on his hip, and he took his Winchester from his saddle scabbard. He didn't know which weapon he would end up using, but he was equally proficient with both.

Across the river in Council Bluffs, Barlowe had a little house, and inside the house he had a wife and a three-year-old daughter. His wife had no idea what he did for a living, and during the four years they'd been married she had never questioned him. When he took a job he made sure that it would never keep him away from home for more than two days. When he got back he had money, and his wife never asked how he'd earned it. Sometimes he thought she knew, and that was why she didn't ask. Other times he just figured she didn't care what he did, as long as they were happy.

He knew if he didn't get out of this business soon the day would come when he wouldn't be able to go back. He'd be dead. He knew he was taking a chance with Clint Adams. A man didn't live as long as Adams had, with the reputation he had, without being good. If he killed Adams, though, the payoff would be worth it.

If Adams killed him . . . well, there'd be a woman and a small girl who would wonder for a long time where he was.

Maybe then his wife would even wonder what he did for his money.

ELEVEN

Clint walked around Omaha for an hour or so, but found that he was looking and not seeing. He finally decided to stop for dinner, and found himself one block from one of the restaurants on the desk clerk's list. He went in and had a bowl of beef stew for dinner that was good—not the best he'd ever had, but good.

Sitting at a table in the back of the small restaurant with his back to the wall, he was able to stare out the window while he ate. That was when he became aware of the man across the street. He was standing in a doorway, not doing anything. He wasn't shopping, and he didn't appear to be waiting for anyone. He appeared to be watching the restaurant that Clint was eating in.

Clint became annoyed with himself. He was being watched, and had probably been followed, and he'd been so preoccupied that he hadn't noticed. He could be dead now and have never seen it coming.

This realization ruined his dinner, and he had to assure the motherly waitress that it wasn't the fault of the food that he hadn't finished eating.

He had more coffee and decided that instead of being the watched, he would become the watcher. He called the waitress over.

"Is there a back door?"

"Why yes, but—"

"There's a man out front who I don't want to run into," he said. "Do you mind if I go out the back?"

"Well . . ."

He took out some money to pay the bill, and then some extra for her.

"All right. It's this way."

"Thank you."

"It's actually a side door, not a back door."

"That'll do."

He followed her through the kitchen, where he drew an odd look from the man who was doing the cooking. He wondered idly why the cooks in most restaurants and cafés were men. Were men actually better cooks than women?

"Thank you," he told her again and stepped out into an alley alongside the restaurant.

He walked to the front of the alley and peered around the corner. The man was still in the doorway across the street. Once or twice, while Clint was watching from inside, the man had to move aside to let someone in or out of the store. Now, while Clint watched, the proprietor came out and said something to the man. In a few seconds they were having a heated exchange, and finally the man stepped out of the doorway. The proprietor said something else sharply and went back inside.

Now the man was out in the open, and clearly nervous about it. He stared across the street at the restaurant, as if trying to see in the window. Clint wondered how long it would take him to figure out that something was wrong.

Something was wrong.

Castle was annoyed that the store owner had come out and made him leave the shelter of the doorway. Now he was out in the open, where Clint Adams could see him if he came out of the restaurant.

Castle was undecided about what to do, so he just stood there staring at the front of the restaurant. He was trying to see in through the window, but the printing on the glass was blocking his view. What if Adams had left while he was arguing with the store owner? No, that couldn't happen. He hadn't turned his head long enough for that to have happened.

Had he?

He decided to give it a little more time, and if Adams didn't come out he was going to cross over and actually peer in the window.

How much more time, he wondered, should he give it?

It took twenty minutes.

Clint noticed the man continually squinting at the

front of the restaurant. Finally he gave up, walked across, and peered in the window. He looked, and looked, then looked again just to make sure—and then he went inside. Clint waited, and the man came out within seconds, looking both ways on the street. Clint ducked back to avoid being seen, then peeked around the corner again. The man was standing there with his hands on his hips, shaking his head, probably wondering how Clint could have gotten by him. Clint hoped that he would assume it had happened while he was arguing with the store owner, and that he would not guess that there was another way out of the restaurant.

Clint waited while the man decided what he should do. Finally, he started walking back the way Clint had come. Clint followed, even though he figured the man was probably going back to the hotel, hoping to pick up his trail again, fresh.

Clint had decided simply to follow the man and not brace him—not yet anyway. Maybe he'd be able to find out who the man was working for without letting anyone know that he was aware he was being watched.

Following the man at a safe distance, Clint first wondered if this could have anything to do with Anne Archer's disappearance—or failure to appear—and then he thought: How *could* it have something to do with her? Who knew he was there meeting her, and looking for her, beyond the two desk clerks and the sheriff? No, he decided—or guessed—that someone must have recognized him, and the man either was following him on his own or had been hired to do so.

He hoped that the observer—who had now become the observed—would lead him to the answer himself.

TWELVE

The man led Clint—as expected—back to the Nebraska Inn. He took up a position across the street after looking undecided. Clint guessed that he must have been weighing whether or not to go into the hotel to check and see if he was there. Clint remained about half a block down, on the hotel side of the street, and waited. He wanted to go inside, but he was afraid he'd miss something if he did. As it turned out, his patience paid off.

Castle saw the man crossing the street toward him and looked away, avoiding his eyes.

Henry Barlowe scared the shit out of him almost as much as Clint Adams did.

"Castle," Barlowe said, "where the hell have you been?"

"I, uh, followed Adams."

"Where'd he go?"

"For a walk."

"Where?"

"He just walked for a while, and then went into a restaurant to eat."

Barlowe waited and when no further information was forthcoming he said, "And then what?"

Castle said something he didn't catch.

"What? What was that?"

"I said . . . I lost him."

Barlowe stared at him.

"How did you manage to do that?"

"I don't know," Castle said, looking at Barlowe for the first time. "He was in the restaurant, and then he wasn't."

"Did you go inside?"

"Yeah, he wasn't in there."

"Did you check for another way out?"

Castle didn't answer. He looked away again.

Barlowe sighed.

"You didn't, did you?"

"No."

Barlowe looked around, across the street, up and down.

"What's wrong?" Castle asked.

"You idiot," Barlowe said. "He probably spotted you and followed you back here."

"Naw," Castle said, frowning. "Why would he follow me? Why wouldn't he go up against me?"

"Because he'd want to know if you're on your own, or if you've been hired by somebody."

Now Castle looked up and down the street.

"Do you think so?"

"I know so," Barlowe said.

"What do we do?"

"We don't do anything," Barlowe said. "You go home."

"I should go and talk to—"

"Go home," Barlowe said, "don't go anyplace else. Go home."

"W-what if he follows me home?"

"If he follows you," Barlowe said, "I'll follow him."

"C-can you take him, Barlowe?"

The man just stared at him.

"I'll go home."

"Go," Barlowe said, "and don't come around here anymore. Understand?"

"Believe me," Castle said, "you don't have to tell me twice."

"Good."

Castle stepped out of the doorway, looked around nervously, and then started off down the block. Barlowe stared after him, shaking his head. By now Clint Adams knew what he looked like. There was only one way to play this now, thanks to the other man's ineptitude.

He stepped out of the doorway, walked across to the hotel, and entered the lobby.

Clint watched as the two men exchanged words. The second man seemed in charge. Whatever he was saying to the first man was embarrassing for him.

Also, Clint could see by his posture that the first man was afraid of the second man.

He could also tell by their postures that the second man was there to do more than just follow him. He wore a gun and he wore it well. He looked to be in his thirties, so he was probably good at what he did.

As Clint watched, both men began looking around. Undoubtedly the second man had just told the first man that he'd probably been followed. Moments later the first man stepped out of the doorway and hurried away, nervously. There was no point in following him. The second man would have told him to go home, or go anywhere but back to the man who'd hired him.

Clint watched the second man now and wasn't surprised when he saw him cross the street and go into the hotel. He'd apparently decided that he'd been spotted and the only approach to take was a straightforward one.

Clint decided to take the very same approach. He stepped from his cover, walked to the hotel, and entered the lobby.

THIRTEEN

As Clint entered the hotel, he saw the other man going into the bar. That surprised him. He had thought the man would wait in the lobby for him and brace him there.

He walked over to the front desk.

"Bob, did you see the man who just came in?"

"Couldn't miss him."

"Do you know him?"

"Sure. His name's Henry Barlowe—only he don't like to be called Henry. He prefers Hank."

"Who is he? I mean, what is he?"

Bob leaned his elbows on the desk.

"You ask me, he's a killer."

"Has he got a reputation?"

"Not like you have," Bob said. "What I mean is, he's known around here, but not much anywhere else—and I think he likes it that way."

49

"Is he good?"

"He's still alive."

Clint nodded. That was an answer he was familiar with.

"Are you, uh, gonna have some business with him?" Bob asked.

"I might," Clint said. "Do you know if he does most of his work for one person?"

Bob shook his head.

"I don't know who he works for. I just figured he worked for whoever paid him."

Clint stared over at the entrance to the bar.

"You gonna brace him in here?"

"I don't know what I'm going to do," Clint said. "I really don't have time to waste."

"That's right," Bob said. "You're leavin' tomorrow for Lincoln, to look for your friend."

"That's right."

Clint was undecided what to do. He could confront Barlowe now, or ignore him and wonder if he was on his trail during the ride to Lincoln. Or he could go to the sheriff now and talk to him about Barlowe.

The third option seemed his best at the moment.

"Hey!" Bob said, as Clint turned and walked toward the door. "What are ya gonna do?"

But Clint kept going out the door and over to the sheriff's office. He never got there, though, because as he approached it he saw the lawman leave and start across the street.

FOURTEEN

"Sheriff Macy!"

The man stopped at the sound of his name and looked around.

"Glad I caught you," Clint said, coming up alongside the man.

"I was just going to make my rounds," Macy said. "Want to walk along?"

"Why not?"

"What can I do for you this time?" the sheriff asked as they started walking.

"You can tell me about a man named Barlowe."

"Hank Barlowe?" Macy asked, surprised. "Do you know him?"

"I never heard of him until today."

"Why today?"

"He's at my hotel."

Macy rubbed a hand over his face.

"That doesn't sound like a coincidence."

"I don't believe in coincidence."

"Neither do I."

"Does he live here?"

"He lives across the river, in Council Bluffs. He only comes to this side of the river for . . . for business."

"And what's his business?"

"Killing."

"And you let him do it?"

"I don't *let* him," Macy said, "I just can't stop him, not if he does it fairly, face-to-face."

"He's good, then?"

"Oh, he's very good," Macy said. "He doesn't have a big reputation, but I think he's done that on purpose. Except for Council Bluffs and Omaha, I'll bet he can go anywhere without being recognized."

"What about Lincoln?"

Macy thought a moment.

"Well, okay, maybe Lincoln, too. Wait a minute." Macy put his hand out to stop their progress and turned to face Clint. "Do you think Barlowe is involved in your friend's disappearance?"

"I don't know."

"Why would you think that?"

"I said I don't know," Clint repeated, "but I'll tell you what I do think."

"What?"

"He's here for me."

"Now why would you think that?"

"Coincidence, remember?" Clint asked. "You said

you didn't believe in it either."

"Yes, but do you know anyone in Omaha?"

"Not a soul."

"I don't think Barlowe would come here for you himself, and how would he know you were here, anyway?"

"He would if someone hired him."

"But you just said you don't know anyone here."

"That's right, but someone knows me."

"Why do you say that?"

"Because they had someone following me today."

"Now how do you know that?"

Clint told the sheriff about seeing the man, then following him back to the hotel, and then seeing him together with Barlowe.

They started walking again while he was talking, Macy listening quietly.

"What did the man following you look like?"

"Average, not very big, not impressive. I don't think he wanted to do what he was doing—and he was very frightened of Barlowe."

"Could be a lot of people," Macy said, but Clint had a feeling he was thinking more than that.

"But?"

Macy hesitated, then said, "It sounds like it could be Willie Castle."

"Who's Willie Castle?"

"Just a man who does odd jobs around Omaha."

"For who?"

"Oh, lots of people."

"But primarily for who?"

Macy hesitated again, longer this time.

"Come on, Sheriff. Somebody's got a tail on me, I'd like to know why."

"Willie does a lot of his work for a man named Michael Percy."

"And who is this Percy?"

"Big man around here," Macy said. "He's a businessman with his fingers in a lot of pies."

"Why would he have someone following me?"

"And why would he hire Barlowe to, uh . . ."

"Kill me?"

"Uh, yes."

"I don't have time to find this stuff out, Sheriff," Clint said. "I've got to get going to Lincoln tomorrow, and I'd like to do it without this Barlowe on my trail."

"Can't say I blame you. Let me guess. You want me to talk to him?"

"I'd rather do it myself," Clint said, "but like I said . . ."

"That's okay," Macy said. "It's my job, anyway. Is he at your hotel now?"

Clint nodded.

"In the bar."

"Let's go."

"Does he know you?"

Macy nodded.

"Mr. Barlowe and I have talked before."

Clint was impressed that Macy was willing to intercede. He'd been afraid the sheriff would regard it as none of his business.

He was liking Sheriff Macy better all the time.

FIFTEEN

When Clint walked into the hotel with the sheriff, Bob looked at them from behind the desk in surprise. Clint thought he detected a look of disappointment, as well, but he couldn't afford to be concerned about that. Whether or not Bob thought he should have brought the sheriff into this was of no concern.

"Bob," the sheriff asked, "is Barlowe still at the bar?"

"Yes, sir, he sure is, Sheriff."

Macy turned to Clint.

"I'd better go in alone."

"Are you sure?"

"If you're there it might antagonize him."

Clint wasn't sure he should let the sheriff go and talk to Barlowe alone.

"Clint," Macy said, "this is nothing I haven't done

before. I'm just gonna talk to him."

"I'll wait here, then."

"I think you'd better wait in your room."

Oddly, Clint felt like a small boy being sent to his room.

"Sheriff—"

"Did you want my help with this or not?"

"Well . . . sure, but—"

"Well, then, we'll do it my way, huh?"

"Sure, okay, Sheriff."

Clint and Bob watched as the sheriff walked over to the door to the saloon and entered. Clint then noticed Bob staring at him.

"I'll be upstairs."

"Sure."

"What's wrong?" Clint asked.

"Nothing."

"Come on, Bob. Spit it out."

"I just never thought you'd go to the sheriff for help."

"What did you expect?"

Bob shrugged.

"Did you want me to go in there and shoot it out with him?"

Bob didn't answer.

"If I did that, he'd be dead now."

"You're so sure of that?"

"That I'd kill him?" Clint asked. "Oh, yes, Bob, there's no doubt."

"Then why did you go to the sheriff?"

"Because I don't *want* to kill anyone, Bob. Is

that so hard to understand?"

From the look on the young man's face, it was.

"Jesus," Clint said to him, "grow up."

With that he turned and went upstairs.

SIXTEEN

Hank Barlowe saw Sheriff Macy approaching him as he stood at the bar with a beer. He was surprised that Clint Adams had gone to the law, but since he'd already decided to play it straight with Adams, he wouldn't do it any different with Macy.

"I'm a little surprised," Barlowe said when the lawman reached him.

"Why's that?"

"I didn't think Adams would go to the law."

"I guess that just points out the difference between you and him, Barlowe."

"You mean that I'm man enough to fight my own fights?" Barlowe asked.

Macy laughed.

"No, that he's smarter than you are."

"You think so?"

"I know so," Macy said. "Actually, you're pretty lucky."

"Why's that?"

"If Clint Adams had walked in here," Macy said, "you probably never would have walked out."

"We have a difference of opinion on that, Sheriff."

"If that's true then you're kidding yourself, Barlowe," Macy said. "You're no match for Clint Adams."

"Because he's got a big rep and I don't?"

"No," Macy said, "because he's better."

For a moment Macy thought Barlowe was going to start shouting. His face turned red and he looked down into his beer mug.

"I don't have any argument with you, Sheriff," he finally said.

"And you do with Adams?"

Barlowe didn't answer.

"You're working for hire, aren't you, Hank? Who's paying you?"

"Nobody."

"Percy?"

Barlowe couldn't lie with his eyes.

"What's Percy's argument with Adams?"

"Damned if I know."

"You'll just kill him for the money, huh?"

"Why, Sheriff," Barlowe said, "I don't kill people for money. You know that."

"I know I've never been able to prove it," Macy said, "but that's all I know."

"Why are you here, Sheriff?"

"A couple of reasons," Macy said. "First, it's my job. Second, I'm tryin' to save your life."

"Goddamn it!" Barlowe said, slamming the beer mug down on the bar. It shattered. Beer and glass showered all over, but somehow he escaped without a cut hand. "What are you tryin' to do, talkin' to me that way? Get yourself killed?"

"You wouldn't kill me, Barlowe."

"Oh? And why not?"

"Because that'd be breaking the law," Macy said, "and you haven't done that yet—not that I can prove."

"Well," Barlowe said, "if I was to kill you now, you wouldn't be able to prove anything then either, would you? You wouldn't be around."

"There are witnesses here, Barlowe."

Barlowe laughed.

"You think anyone here would say anything? Besides, it'd be a fair fight, wouldn't it?"

"I'm not gonna draw on you, Henry—"

Suddenly Barlowe swung. His fist collided with the lawman's jaw, sending him staggering back. Macy's hat flew from his head as the man fought to retain his balance.

"Don't call me that!" Barlowe screamed.

"Damn you, Barlowe," Macy said.

Onlookers' opinions would differ later on. Half of the people in the bar would swear they saw Sheriff Macy go for his gun. Others would say that he simply took a step toward Barlowe, saying, "You're under arrest—"

Everyone agreed, though, that Barlowe drew quickly and fired once. The bullet struck Macy in the chest, where his heart was. He staggered under the impact, stopped for a moment, then sank slowly to his knees and toppled onto his face.

Barlowe holstered his gun and looked around the bar.

"You better leave, Hank," the bartender said.

Barlowe swung around and looked at the man, who took a step back. He didn't want to leave, but he knew the bartender was right, and he knew he'd made a mistake. He'd let his temper get the better of him. He had to go someplace, calm down and think this through.

"If anyone says it wasn't a fair fight . . ." he said, looking around.

No one spoke.

Barlowe looked down at the sheriff, then stepped over the body and left. As Barlowe walked through the lobby, Bob stared after him, wondering what had happened, afraid that he already knew.

Upstairs Clint heard the shot and was out of his room quickly. He ran down the stairs to the lobby and looked at Bob.

"What happened?"

"You better go in and see for yourself," Bob said.

Clint's heart was in his throat as he crossed the lobby and entered the bar.

SEVENTEEN

Clint sat in the sheriff's office across the desk from the deputy. His name was Paul Young, and Clint hadn't even known he existed until after Sheriff Macy was killed.

"Tell it to me again," Young said.

"I've told it to you six times already, Deputy," Clint said. He wanted to ask the man where he had been when the sheriff was getting killed, but that wouldn't have been fair. It was his fault, not the deputy's.

Clint had rushed from the lobby into the bar, only to almost trip over the body of the sheriff. Moments later the deputy had come running in, asking what had happened. No one in the bar offered a reply.

Clint was the only one talking.

"Why don't you question the witnesses?" Clint asked in the sheriff's office.

"I have," the deputy said, "and none of them will say they saw anything."

"That's ridiculous," Clint said. "The sheriff went in there to talk to Barlowe."

"Did you see Barlowe in the saloon?" Deputy Young asked. His name was appropriate, because he was probably not yet twenty-five.

"No."

"And no one else will say they did."

"What about the desk clerk?"

"Him, neither." Young pointed at Clint and said, "You're the only one who says Hank Barlowe was around."

"So if he wasn't, who killed the sheriff?"

"That's what I want to know."

"I'm telling you who killed him," Clint said. "Hank Barlowe."

"Why?"

"I don't know why."

"But you say Barlowe was after you?"

"Yes."

"So why didn't you go in and talk to him?"

"I explained that to you already."

The deputy, who was probably doing a remarkable job, given his youth, sat back and said, "Tell it to me again."

Clint sighed. For three hours he'd gone over and over it with the deputy, mentioning Barlowe and the man Sheriff Macy had talked about, Percy. The deputy listened to him tell it one more time and then said he didn't know what he could do about any of it.

"I have no witnesses."

"Talk to Percy."

That was the only time the deputy backed off.

"You can go now, Mr. Adams."

"Deputy—"

"I'll be talking to the, uh, witnesses again tomorrow, but whatever happened, they're not talking."

"They're all afraid of Henry Barlowe."

"That may be," the deputy said, "but unless one of them tells me Barlowe was there, I can't even question him."

"I saw him there."

"You saw him go into the hotel, you said, you didn't see him in the saloon."

Exasperated, Clint stood up and left the office.

Back at the hotel he saw that Bob was no longer behind the desk. There was a man there he didn't know, a tall, thin man with a sallow complexion and droopy eyes.

"Where's Bob?" he asked.

"He ain't here tonight."

"Why not?"

The man shrugged and his eyes almost closed. Clint didn't know if he was sleepy or if his eyes were always like that.

"I don't know," the man said. "All I know is I was told I got to work."

"Do you know where he lives?"

"No. I only work here part of the time, when they need me . . . like tonight."

Clint didn't know what else to ask so he went up

to his room. He removed his gun belt and hung it on the bedpost, then pulled off his boots. He dropped the second boot to the floor and then just sat there. There was no doubt in his mind that he had gotten the sheriff killed, but what could he do about it now? He had to leave for Lincoln in the morning. His first concern had to be Anne Archer. Once he found her, he could come back to Omaha and look for Hank Barlowe. On the other hand, Hank Barlowe might still come looking for him. There was no way of knowing.

He put his feet up on the bed and sat with his back against the headboard. He should have gone to talk to Barlowe himself. Why hadn't he? In the past he'd always taken care of his own business. Was he afraid that Barlowe might have killed him? No, he could honestly say he didn't do what he did out of fear. He was trying to avoid trouble so that he could continue to look for Anne Archer the next day. His concern had been for her, and it still was. He felt sorry for the sheriff, but the man himself had put it to him that he was doing his job. When you wore a badge, you wore a target on your chest. Clint had decided that years ago, and he still felt the same way.

The sheriff had known what he was doing. Clint had to believe that.

Still, he wished at least one person would come forward and say what had happened.

EIGHTEEN

In the morning Clint rose early and left the hotel to go to the livery. He didn't bother with breakfast. He had no appetite.

The first clerk he'd met upon his arrival in town was behind the desk. Apparently, he'd heard that something had happened the night before, because he gave Clint a frightened look. Clint thought the man was going to bolt and run.

Although he had made arrangements with Bob to hold his room, he decided not to check with this man if that would still be the case. He'd find out when he returned.

He left the hotel and walked to the livery. As he approached, he saw Deputy Young waiting there with four other men, none of whom were wearing badges.

"Good morning, Deputy," Clint said.

The man didn't answer.

"What can I do for you?"

"I understand you're leaving today."

"That's right."

"Comin' back?"

"I don't know yet."

The deputy shook his head.

"I don't think you should."

"And why is that?"

"We don't need no trouble here."

"Have I caused trouble, Deputy?"

"The sheriff's dead."

"That was because of Henry Barlowe."

"You say."

"You think I killed the sheriff?"

"I don't know who killed the sheriff, Adams," Young said. "I'm just tellin' you not to come back here."

Clint looked around at the other four men.

"Are these men here to back your play?"

Young looked surprised. He suddenly clasped his hands behind his back.

"I ain't makin' no play." His voice shook, betraying his nervousness.

"Relax, Deputy," Clint said. "I'm not going to draw on you." Clint was holding his rifle in one hand and his saddlebags in the other. He would have had to drop those before going for his gun. He had no doubt that he could do that, but he certainly had no *intentions* of doing it.

"I'm telling you this for your own good, Adams,"

the deputy said. "Don't come back here."

"And I'm telling you," Clint said. "If I don't find what I'm after in Lincoln, I have no choice but to come back here."

"That would be a mistake."

Clint stared at the deputy for a few moments, then looked at the other four.

"You men can go."

They exchanged glances, then looked at the deputy.

"The deputy doesn't need you."

Still unsure, they shuffled their feet.

"Go!" Clint shouted. The men jumped and began moving away.

"Go on, you can leave," the deputy said. It was false bravado on his part, giving them permission to do what they were already doing. With the permission, though, the men walked away faster.

"There was no need for this, Deputy. What did you think I was going to do?"

The man didn't answer.

"Who put you up to this?"

Still no answer.

"Come on."

"Nobody."

"You decided to do this on your own?"

"That's right."

"Who told you I was leaving?"

"Fingers."

That could have been true.

"I've got some advice for you. If you're smart you'll take it."

The man said nothing, but he made no move to leave.

"If you're going to take over Macy's job, don't let anyone tell you how to do it—not even if he's a successful businessman. The law doesn't fit in anyone's pockets, son."

"I never said—"

"Second, while I'm gone, talk to the desk clerk at the hotel, Bob. I believe his uncle owns the hotel. Do you know him?"

"I know Bob."

"Good. He saw Barlowe arrive and leave, and we talked about it."

"He said he didn't see anything."

"Pressure him," Clint said. "Lie to him if you have to."

"What kind of lie?" the deputy asked, interested in spite of himself.

"Tell him someone else talked and now you know Barlowe was there. He saw him enter, heard the shot, and saw him leave. He'll talk to you."

The deputy digested that, then looked at Clint and asked, "What else?" The question made Clint think there was hope for the young man yet.

"Don't go near Barlowe if you see him," Clint said. "Wait until I come back."

"But if he did kill the sheriff—"

"Don't go near him," Clint said again. "You're no match for him. Understand?"

After a moment the deputy said, "I understand."

"And don't think that men like those four will help you."

Clint walked past the deputy then and into the livery. The deputy, unsure what to do, stood outside the livery for a few moments, but by the time Clint came out leading Duke he was gone. Clint mounted up, hoping that the man would heed his warning and take his advice.

He left Omaha and rode toward Lincoln.

NINETEEN

It took Clint longer than he expected to get to Lincoln because he kept stopping to check his back trail. If Henry "Hank" Barlowe was going to try him, he didn't want to get surprised.

When he rode into Lincoln it was dark. The town was much smaller than Omaha, and the streets at this time of the evening were almost deserted. He did find a man crossing the street, though, and asked him where the sheriff's office was. He rode Duke over to it and dismounted. He knocked on the door and entered.

"Hello," he said to the man behind the desk.

"Hi," the man, a deputy, answered. "Can I help ya?"

He was in his thirties, probably a more experienced deputy than Paul Young from Omaha.

"I'm looking for Sheriff Chadwick."

71

"You missed him," the deputy said. "He went home an hour ago."

"Oh . . . well, can you tell me where he lives?"

"Not if I want to keep my job—and my scalp—I can't." The man's tone was good-natured, but Clint didn't think he was going to get anything out of him.

"When will he be in, then?"

"Tomorrow morning, early."

"All right," Clint said. "I'll check in with him then." He started for the door.

"Hey, can I say who was here?"

"No," Clint said. "I'll come back in the morning and introduce myself then. Thanks for your help."

As Clint went out the door, the deputy, whose name was Ted Phelan, frowned. There was something familiar about the man, but he couldn't place it.

He opened the top drawer of the desk, took out a stack of wanted posters, and started going through them.

Clint left the sheriff's office and walked Duke over to the nearest hotel. He left him outside again and went in to get a room.

"Gonna be stayin' long?" the clerk asked. Desk clerks were starting to blur for Clint. This one was heavyset, in his forties.

"I don't know," he said, signing the book. "I understand you've been having some trouble here."

"Trouble? Oh, you must mean the murder."

"That's right, the murder."

"That's no trouble," the man said. "The sheriff can handle that."

"Is that so?"

"Yup."

The man turned to get Clint his key, and Clint realized that he wasn't going to say much more on the subject.

"Here you go, sir, number ten."

Clint took the key.

"I heard it was a woman who was killed."

"That's right, it was, but that seemed to be fitting."

"What do you mean?"

"Well, according to the sheriff," the clerk said, "it was also a woman who killed her."

"You don't say."

"That's what he said."

"And he's got the woman—the killer—in jail, has he?" Clint asked.

"No," the man said, "but he says he knows who did it, and it's only a matter of time before he brings her in."

"I guess he must be a pretty good lawman, huh?"

"Sheriff Chadwick?" the clerk said. "He's the best lawman we ever had here in Lincoln. The best."

"I guess you're very lucky, then," Clint said. "Uh, could you direct me to the nearest livery?"

TWENTY

Clint took Duke to a livery stable close by and told the liveryman he wouldn't be staying more than a day or two. After that he tried to find someplace to get something to eat, but most of the places were closed. He finally stopped into a saloon for a beer and talked to the bartender about something to eat.

"I don't know," the man said, "I could probably find you a sandwich, or some hard-boiled eggs."

"Anything would do," Clint said.

"Let me see what I can do. Take a table." The man started away, then turned back. "It won't be cheap."

"I'll pay," Clint said, "within reason."

The bartender thought it over, then nodded and went off to see what he could do. Clint turned, saw an empty table against the wall, and claimed it. This particular saloon didn't offer much beyond drinks and a couple of bored-looking girls walking around the floor. There was no gaming going on, so it was only about half full. That suited Clint fine. He had chosen it because it wasn't too noisy.

When the bartender came out he was carrying a tray with a sandwich and a small bowl of hard-boiled eggs. Two men tried to get something from him as he passed, but he pulled away from them.

"Here ya go," he said, putting the food down on the table. "We had some baloney, and the eggs ain't *too* old."

"It's fine," Clint said. He took out some money and paid far more than the food was worth.

The bartender looked surprised.

"For this you got another beer coming."

"Bring it."

Clint's first instinct was to lift the bread and look at the meat inside, but he decided he was too hungry for that. He took a bite and washed it down with a mouthful of beer. Then he peeled an egg, discarded it, peeled another and ate it. He washed that down with some more beer.

"Here ya go," the bartender said, putting another beer on the table. "How's the food?"

Clint gave him a look.

"Okay, never mind. I guess I'm pushing it."

"Got a minute to sit down?" Clint asked.

"What for?"

"Some conversation."

"About what?"

"Murder."

"You know," the man said, "if I wasn't a bartender I wouldn't do this."

The man sat down. He had a bald head and a pitted face that seemed to be covered with hair: a mustache, some heavy stubble, and dark, heavy eyebrows.

"What's being a bartender got to do with it?" Clint asked.

"It's in the bartender's code," the man said. "If I tend bar I got to listen to what people say."

Clint laughed and asked, "What's your name?"

"Fred."

"Fred what?"

The man shrugged.

"Just Fred. I give my customers my last name they might figure out where I live."

"Why would they do that?"

"I'm a good listener . . . but I only listen on the job. What is it you want me to listen to?"

"I was hoping to listen to you."

"About what? The merits of Lincoln, Nebraska?"

"I understand a woman was killed here a few days ago."

"Last week, more like it."

"I saw an old newspaper," Clint said. "I'm not sure of the date."

"Last week, it was."

"How was she killed?"

"Her throat was cut."

"Did anyone know her?"

Fred shook his head.

"She was a stranger in town."

Clint got a cold feeling in the pit of his stomach.

He pushed the bowl away with three eggs still in it, his appetite gone.

"Don't want those eggs?"

Clint decided to be frank with the bartender.

"Fred, I'm here looking for a woman."

"Well, you don't want one of these. Tired specimens, they are. I can tell you where to go . . . but it won't be cheap."

"No, I'm looking for a specific woman . . . one person in particular."

"Oh, I misunderstood. Who is she?"

"Her name's Anne Archer."

"Don't know her."

"A very beautiful red-haired woman."

"I've seen a few of those."

"She wears a gun and works as a bounty hunter."

For a moment Clint thought he saw something in Fred's eyes, a flicker of recognition.

"Fred . . ."

"I think I saw a woman like that," the bartender said.

"Where? When?"

"Here in town, last week."

"Fred, she wasn't the one who was killed, was she?"

"I didn't see the girl who was killed, mister. I can't say. What did you say your name was?"

"I didn't . . . but it's Adams, Clint Adams."

Now there was a definite look of recognition on the man's face.

"Jesus, you're—"

"Looking for a woman named Anne Archer."

Fred fell silent and stared at Clint for a few moments before answering.

"I can't say I saw a woman by that name, but I did see an attractive red-haired woman wearing a gun."

"Where?"

Fred waved a hand and said, "Out there, somewhere on the street. I saw her walking."

"Was there anyone with her?"

"Not when I saw her."

"Did anyone else see her?"

"I don't know."

"Where did you see her?"

"I can't remember. Somewhere around here."

"Near the bar?"

The big man stood up.

"I got to get back to work."

Clint looked over at the bar and saw that no one was standing at it.

"Doesn't look like you're very busy."

"I got to get ready to close up."

"Well, thanks for the food and the beer."

"You paid for them."

"And the conversation."

"I didn't tell you much," Fred said, his eyes darting around. "In fact, I didn't tell you nothing helpful, did I? Well, did I?"

"No, Fred," Clint said, because he thought the man wanted to hear it, "nothing helpful at all."

TWENTY-ONE

Clint woke at first light the next morning and got dressed. He didn't know how early the sheriff would arrive at his office, but he wanted to be there when he did. He stopped in the hotel dining room for coffee, but did not take time for breakfast. When he got to the sheriff's office he found it locked. It reminded him of waiting for Sheriff Macy in Omaha, and that made him think of Macy being killed by Barlowe. That made him feel badly about it all over again. He wondered if he shouldn't have stayed in Omaha and gone after Barlowe. What if Anne simply decided not to keep their appointment for some innocent reason? What if she was in no danger? No, he decided not to believe that. It would mean that the sheriff had died for nothing.

"Can I help you?"

He looked up and saw a man with a badge standing

a few feet away. He was in his early forties, square-jawed and handsome, with wide shoulders and narrow hips. Clint thought that the cleft in the man's chin probably made him a favorite with the women in Lincoln.

"You're blocking my door," the man said.

"Sheriff Chadwick?"

"If I wasn't, this wouldn't be my door, would it? Do you mind?"

Clint stepped aside to allow the man to unlock the door.

"My name is Clint Adams."

Chadwick pushed his door open but did not go through the doorway. He turned his head to look at Clint.

"You sent the telegram from Omaha."

"That's right."

"You've got a lot of nerve," Chadwick said and went inside. Clint followed.

"What do you mean by that?"

Chadwick walked to his desk and stood behind it.

"You're not a lawman. How dare you send me a telegram asking for information."

"If I'd had Sheriff Macy send it, would you have replied differently?"

"No."

"Why?"

"Macy is a joke as a lawman."

Clint didn't agree.

"Well, nobody will be laughing anymore."

"What do you mean?"

"Macy was shot and killed yesterday."

Chadwick didn't speak for a moment, then he looked down.

"I'm sorry to hear that. I didn't like him, or respect him, but I'm sorry he's dead." He finally sat down. "Who did it?"

"There's some question about that. May I sit down?"

Chadwick replied with a wave of his hand.

"What do you mean, some question?"

"There were witnesses," Clint said, "but no one will admit to seeing who did it."

Chadwick studied Clint for a moment.

"But you know, don't you? Or think you do?"

"I know."

"All right," Chadwick said, after another moment, "who?"

"Do you know a man named Henry Barlowe?"

"Hank Barlowe," Chadwick said, nodding, "I know him. Why would he kill Macy?"

"I'm afraid that was my fault."

"How so?"

"To explain that I'd have to start at the beginning."

"Is this a long story?"

"It could be."

"I'd better make some coffee, then."

TWENTY-TWO

Chadwick listened patiently and supplied Clint with a cup of coffee when it was ready. He didn't speak until Clint was finished.

"Well, first of all, the woman who was killed did not have red hair, she had black hair."

"She wasn't an Indian, was she?" Clint asked, thinking of Katy Littlefeather.

"No, she wasn't."

"What else can you tell me?"

"Nothing."

"Why not?"

"As I said before, Mr. Adams, you are not an officer of the law."

"I'm not looking to interfere with your job in any way, Sheriff. I'm just trying to locate my friend."

Chadwick fell silent and stared down at his coffee

cup. Clint decided to wait the man's thought processes out.

"Well, I think I'm looking for your friend, too, Mr. Adams," Chadwick finally said.

"What do you mean?"

"I mean according to my information the dead woman was killed by another woman . . . a red-haired woman."

Clint's relief that Anne wasn't dead turned to shock that she might be considered the killer.

"Why would she ask you to meet her in Omaha, Mr. Adams?"

"I don't know," Clint said. "She didn't say why in her telegram."

"Then why would you come all this way to meet her?" Chadwick asked.

"Because we're friends, Sheriff."

"Close friends?"

"Very good friends."

The two men stared at each other for a few moments.

"Mr. Adams, you wouldn't be here to help her elude me, would you? If you were, that wouldn't be a wise course of action for you to take."

"It seems to me," Clint said slowly, "that she's done a good job all by herself of eluding you up till now."

Chadwick looked stung.

"That's only temporary," the lawman said.

"What if she's already gone?"

Chadwick shook his head.

"I don't think so."

"Why not?"

"Because if she had left here she would have gone to meet you in Omaha, don't you think?"

Clint frowned. That was true enough. If she wasn't in Omaha, and he hadn't encountered her between there and Lincoln, she had to still be here, somewhere.

"I see you agree with me."

"To tell you the truth, Sheriff, I don't know what to think."

"Well, let me give you some advice," Chadwick said. "If she is here, and if you find her, turn her over to me. It would be better for her, and for you."

That sounded odd to Clint.

"Sheriff, let me ask you a question."

"Go ahead," the man said, "but I'm not promising to answer it."

"Who was the woman who was killed?"

Chadwick's face closed up tight.

"That's not important."

"Not important to me, or to you?" Clint asked.

"Not important to anyone," Chadwick said. "It doesn't matter who Miss Archer killed—"

"If she killed anyone."

"What matters is that she is on the run, and I'm going to find her. Then a judge and jury can decide if she killed . . . anyone."

Clint wondered who the dead woman was that her identity was being kept such a secret.

"Has the woman been buried yet?"

"She has."

"Where?"

"That's none of your business."

"What's the big secret, Sheriff?" Clint asked. "Who was the woman?"

"I think I've answered just about enough of your questions, Adams," Chadwick said. "Just remember what I said. If you find your friend, bring her to me."

"Are you so convinced that she killed this mysterious woman that you're not looking elsewhere?"

"Why should I look elsewhere?" Chadwick asked. "She did it."

"Then I guess you have witnesses."

"I have all the witnesses—wait a minute. I told you I've answered all the questions I'm going to."

"Just one more, Sheriff. Do you—"

Chadwick stood up and said, "Get out of my office, Adams!"

Clint stood up very slowly. For the first time in a long time he deliberately tried to intimidate a lawman. He stared at Chadwick for a few moments, but the man did not budge. Either Chadwick didn't care about Clint's reputation, or there was someone the man was even more afraid of.

Without another word Clint turned and left the office.

TWENTY-THREE

Clint spent a good part of the day asking around after Anne but came up with no information. So that night he went back to the saloon. He had the feeling that the bartender, Fred, knew more than he was saying.

When he entered, the place was much busier than it had been the night before when he'd been there. Fred was again behind the bar, though, and Clint went over and found a space he could fit into without too much bumping. Bumping someone at the bar was sometimes the biggest sin you could commit in a saloon.

"You back again?" Fred asked.

"Why wouldn't I be?"

Fred shrugged.

"Thought maybe the sheriff was gonna send you on your way."

"Or lock me up?"

The man shrugged again.

"Did I do something I should be locked up for, Fred?" Clint asked.

"How the hell would I know?" Fred asked. "You want somethin'?"

"A beer would be nice."

"Comin' up."

Clint looked around while he was waiting for his beer. It occurred to him that he was in Fred's place, where Fred had a lot of friends. If he started asking questions the man didn't want to answer, he could be in a lot of trouble.

"Here's your beer."

"Thanks."

Fred stared at Clint as if waiting for him to say something else and then looked vaguely surprised when he didn't.

"Can I do something for you?" Clint asked.

"Uh, no . . ." the bartender said, betraying his confusion.

Clint turned his back to the bar and worked on his beer. Behind him he sensed the bartender moving away.

He was still studying the room, idly watching people as they went through the motions of having their night's fun, when three men entered through the batwing doors and stood just inside. They looked around the room and then one of them nudged another and jerked his head Clint's way. Who had sent them? he wondered. Chadwick? Or someone else?

And why? Because he was asking questions about the dead woman?

"Hey, Fred!"

The bartender came over.

"Another beer?"

"I'm not finished with this one. See those three hard cases by the door?"

Fred looked over there and his face fell.

"Yeah, I see them."

"You know them, don't you?"

"Yeah, I do. You want to use the back door?"

"I don't think so. Tell me, are they here to scare me, bust me up, or kill me?"

Fred studied Clint for a moment, then seemed to decide that he deserved the truth.

"Not to scare you. That's not what they do."

"Hurt me or kill me, then, huh?"

"One of the two."

"Friends of yours?"

Fred blew some air out of his mouth, making a disgusted sound.

"Not likely."

"Okay then, I might need a witness after this. You know, for the sheriff?"

"Uh-huh. You gonna bust up my place?"

"I'm going to try not to."

Fred studied him again, then asked, "You gonna need help?"

"I don't think so."

"I got a greener back here, just in case. You say the word."

"Why?"

Fred shrugged.

"It ain't the way I do business."

"Okay, then," Clint said.

When the other men at the bar saw the three men just inside the door, they seemed to know something was going to happen. They looked around, spotted Clint as the stranger in their midst, and slowly moved away from him.

The hard cases turned to face him, then approached, remaining three abreast.

"You Clint Adams?" the lead man asked.

"That's right."

"We been asked to see you out of town."

"Is that a fact?"

"It is."

"At whose request?"

"Well, as far as you're concerned, ours."

Clint studied the three men for a few seconds. They were of a kind. Their clothes and gun belts were worn, the guns themselves well used but still able to dole out death at a moment's notice.

"I don't think so."

The lead man stared at him, blinked, then said, "What?"

"I said I don't think so. I'm not ready to leave just yet."

"Now, mister," the lead man said, "we ain't askin' you, we are tellin' you."

"Yeah," one of the other men said.

The third one remained quiet. Clint looked at him

harder and decided he'd be the first one to take down—or talk to.

"What's your name?" Clint asked him.

The other two men looked confused and turned to look at the third man.

"Hayes."

"Hayes, why don't you look at me and tell your friends what you see?" Clint suggested.

"What's he talkin' about, Hayes?" the lead man asked.

Hayes didn't answer. He was staring hard at Clint. Finally he spoke to the other two men without moving his eyes.

"I don't think we should do this."

"Hey, Hayes," the first man said, "we're gettin' paid to do this. We can't back down now. You better do what you're gettin' paid to do or be ready to leave town."

Hayes continued to stare at Clint, then shrugged as if to say, "What can I do?"

Clint was sorry the other two men hadn't listened to him.

Everybody in the saloon seemed to know what was going to happen next, because chairs scraped, tables overturned, and men hit the floor.

"You comin'?" the lead man asked.

"I said no," Clint said.

"Your funeral."

"You got that wrong . . ." Clint said.

He switched his beer from his right hand to his left as the three men went for their guns. Almost regretfully he drew and killed Hayes, the fastest of the three by a lot. The other two men still had not quite cleared leather when he shot them each once in the chest.

He holstered his gun and shifted his beer back to his right hand.

"*Your* funeral," he said, looking down at the lead man.

TWENTY-FOUR

"Jesus."

It was Fred speaking. Clint turned and saw the man standing there with the greener shotgun in his hands.

"I guess you didn't need any help, did ya?" Fred asked.

"I might now, though," Clint said. "I have a feeling these men were sent by the sheriff."

"Why would he do that?" Fred asked, putting his shotgun away.

"He's not too happy with me being in town."

"Because you're askin' about that woman who got killed?"

"I think so. Do you know anything about her, Fred?"

"You might want to use the back door, mister," Fred said, instead of answering the question.

"Why?" Clint asked. "Are you not going to back my story?"

"I'll back ya," Fred said. "I seen what happened."

"But you won't answer my questions?"

"I—I can't," Fred said helplessly.

At that moment the sheriff came walking into the saloon. People were still righting tables and sitting back in their chairs as he did so. He looked around, walked over to the dead bodies, checked them and then looked at Clint. He did not look happy.

"Did you do this, Adams?"

"I did."

"Who started it?"

"In spite of my reputation, Sheriff," Clint said, "I don't go around starting gunfights with three men at a time."

"Fred?" Chadwick said, looking past Clint.

Clint held his breath, wondering if the bartender was going to be true to his word.

"It's like he said, Sheriff," Fred said finally. "They came in and pushed him."

The sheriff looked even less happy and gave Fred a hard look before moving his gaze back to Clint.

"I'm going to talk to some of these other people, Adams," he said, "and if I even get one conflicting report I'm going to run you out of town."

"Try."

"What?"

"You mean you're going to try to run me out of town," Clint said. He took a step closer to the law-man. "And if I find out that you sent these men after me, Sheriff, you won't want to be in town. Understand?"

Chadwick swallowed, his eyes moving around nervously. He knew he couldn't back down in front of all these people and he didn't. Clint had to give him credit for that.

The lawman swallowed hard and said, "You can't threaten me in my own town, Adams."

"It's not a threat, Sheriff," Clint said, "you have my word."

Clint turned and put his mug back on the bar.

"Thanks," he said to Fred, for more than the beer.

"Sure," Fred said.

"I'll be in my hotel room," Clint said to Chadwick, "if you want me."

The room was dead quiet as he walked out, but as soon as he went through the batwing doors he heard it erupt in a flurry of activity and voices.

TWENTY-FIVE

Clint slept very little that night. If the sheriff would send three men after him in the saloon, what was to keep him from sending someone to kill him in his hotel room while he slept?

Of course, he didn't know for certain that they were sent by the sheriff, but the man had sure looked disappointed to walk into that saloon after the shooting to find Clint still standing.

He had been in his room for a few hours, still awake, when there was a light, tentative knock on the door. He took his gun from the gun belt hanging on the bedpost and moved to the door.

"Who is it?"

"It's Denise."

"Denise?"

"Come on, let me in. I don't have all night—well, maybe I do. Hey!" It sounded like she started slapping the door with her palm.

Clint unlocked the door and swung it open, gun still in hand.

"What the—" he said, but she shocked him by throwing her arms around him and kissing him soundly. He still hadn't gotten a good look at her, but her lips felt full and soft, and her breath was sweet. Her body, pressed against him, felt full and firm.

She broke the kiss and put her mouth to his ear.

"Fred sent me," she whispered. "Let me in."

She backed away from him then and he got a good look at her. Her impressive bosom was almost spilling out from her low-cut bodice. She had a mass of black hair that fanned out around her head and reached to her shoulders. She stood there with her hands planted on her hips, staring at him.

"Are you gonna let me in, lover?"

"Uh . . . sure, come on in . . . Denise."

"Ooh, sugar," she said, louder than he thought necessary, "you are gonna have yourself one helluva night tonight, I guarantee it."

She marched past him into the room and he closed the door behind them.

"What's going on?" he asked.

"Fred sent me."

"You said that, but for what?"

"He has some information for you, but he couldn't come himself so he sent me. He thought it would look less suspicious if I came up here."

"Why?"

She gave him a look with an arched eyebrow.

"Ain't it obvious? Why else would I be comin' up to your room?"

"I don't recognize you from the saloon."

"That's 'cause I don't work the saloon. I work for Fred, but not there, understand?"

"How do I know you work for Fred?"

"Who else would I work for?"

"How about the sheriff?"

Now she gave him an exasperated look.

"I wouldn't work for that stiff-back on a bet."

"Stiff-back?"

"He thinks he's so much better than the rest of us."

"The rest of who?"

"Us. You, me, Fred, anybody who ain't him."

Her dislike of the sheriff seemed real enough.

"Look, according to Fred you were in the saloon last night and today. You asked him some questions about a red-haired woman? Is she your wife or somethin'?"

"What's the message?"

"Could you put that gun down? Who were you expecting, anyway?"

Clint walked to the bedpost and reholstered the gun, but remained near it. She might have had a cohort outside the room. If somebody kicked the door in, he wanted to be ready.

"What's the message?"

"He said the woman you're lookin' for was here in town."

"I know that. The sheriff told me that much."

"Look, mister—"

"Clint."

"Okay, Clint. I'm just deliverin' a message, and I got to do it in order or I'll forget it."

"Okay, go ahead."

She started from the beginning.

"He says that your lady was in town and got herself mixed up in somethin' she shouldn't have."

"Like what?"

"Like he don't know, but it had something to do with a big shot."

"Who?"

"Fred don't know."

"What does Fred know?"

"You're gonna mix me up again!"

"Okay, but don't start from the beginning again."

She took a few seconds to remember where she was, then started again from there.

"He says the dead woman was a rich man's lady—you know, mistress, on account of he was married? Somebody killed her, and Fred thinks that your lady friend was framed."

"Wait a minute," Clint said. "Are you saying the rich guy—whoever he is—wanted to get rid of her, so he had her killed and had Anne framed for it?"

"Is that her name? Anne?"

"The sheriff must be in on it, because he wants to lock her up. But she gets away."

"That sounds like what Fred thinks."

"Why is Fred telling me all this?"

"The sheriff closed him down after you left." She made a face. "Fred hates the sheriff. I do, too. That's why I said I'd help."

Maybe, since Fred knew who Clint was, he was also afraid of him.

"Did Fred tell you who I am?"

"Well, yeah," she said, turning suddenly shy, "that's another reason I agreed to help."

"You could get into trouble for this, Denise," he said.

"Then maybe you better make it worth my while."

"Huh?"

She reached up and slid the dress off her shoulders and let it drop to the floor. She had a breathtaking body, full and womanly, the skin smooth and pale. Her breasts were very full, with large, dark nipples. Clint felt himself responding in spite of himself.

"Look, Denise—" he started, thinking of Anne Archer.

"Look," she said, interrupting him, "to make this look good I got to stay the night."

Clint took a moment, then said, "That makes sense."

"And if I'm gonna stay the night," she went on, moving closer to him, "we might as well make the most of it."

As she pressed her naked body to him, he could feel her heat right through his clothes.

He said, "That makes sense . . ."

TWENTY-SIX

Denise removed Clint's clothes slowly, first the shirt and then his trousers. He had already removed his boots earlier. When she pulled his shorts down to his ankles she stared at his erection for a moment, then licked her lips and said, "Um."

He stepped out of his shorts and kicked them away. She leaned into him and kissed his belly, then licked her way down to his penis. She circled the head with her tongue a few times, wetting it, then opened her mouth and engulfed him. Her mouth was hot and wet, and while she sucked him she held his testicles in one hand.

"Mmmm," she said as she rode him up and down with her mouth. He reached down to cup her head with his left hand while she ran her other hand around behind him and over his butt. He could see why Fred didn't have her working the saloon but working privately. She certainly knew what she was doing.

He slid his hand down to her neck and then to her back, reaching down as far as he could.

"Oh, God," she said, letting him pop free from her mouth, "I want you in me. . . . "

She pushed him away from the bed and then got on her hands and knees on the mattress.

"This way, I want you this way . . ." she said breathlessly.

He got behind her, grabbed her hips, and pulled her toward the top of the bed, positioning her the way he wanted her. That done, he spread her thighs and slid his erection between them. He found her wet and waiting and drove himself home. He entered her cleanly, and she gasped as he began to move in her. Every time he thrust himself forward, she pushed her butt back against him and moaned. As their tempo increased, the room filled with the sound of their flesh slapping together, faster and faster. She began to sweat and her scent started to permeate the room, joining with his. The room seemed to grow hotter and hotter. Her hair was now sticking to the moist flesh of her back.

"Oh, God, now, come on, come on, now!" she shouted . . . and the door suddenly snapped open from a kick that almost took it off its hinges.

Denise screamed, but Clint grabbed her by the hair with his left hand. With his right he drew his gun from the holster on the bedpost and shot the man who stepped into the room with his gun already drawn. The bullet struck the man in the face, because he came into the room in a crouch. The shot drove him back outside into the hall, where he collapsed.

"Oh, Jesus, oh, Jesus . . ." Denise was shouting.

Still erect and still inside her, Clint maintained his hold on her hair and pulled her head all the way back so he could insert the barrel of the gun in her mouth.

"You want to suck on something, Denise? Suck on this."

"Oh, gahh—" she said around the barrel.

He took the barrel from her mouth and pressed it to her temple.

"Oh, God, mister, don't shoot me, please."

"Tell me who sent you!"

"Fred really sent me, he really did, b-but—" She stopped because her tears were choking her.

"But what?" Clint shouted. He had very little pity for her at this point.

"B-but the sheriff was waiting for me outside. He told me to go ahead and deliver Fred's message, but then I was supposed to have sex with you . . ."

"Do you know why he wanted you to have sex with me?" Clint asked.

"Oh, God, I do now. To keep you busy so that man could shoot you—but I didn't know before, mister. Honest I didn't."

"So everything you told me was the truth?"

"Oh, yes, yes, just the way Fred told me to tell it to you. I swear, mister, please d-don't kill me, I s-swear on my mother's—"

He released her head and said, "Get dressed."

He walked into the hall naked and checked the gunman to make sure he was dead. When she put her dress on, she came to the door.

"Do you know him?" Clint asked.

The bullet had smashed his nose.

"I can't—oh geez, oh, God, I'm gonna be sick—I can't tell—"

He stood up and faced her.

"Go on, get out of here."

"What should I s-say to Fred, and the sheriff?"

"Avoid the sheriff. I'll go and see him myself."

She started down the hall.

"Denise?"

"Yeah?" She turned quickly.

"If I hear you warned him—"

"I ain't gonna warn nobody, mister, honest."

"Then go ahead, get!"

She turned and ran down the hall to the stairway.

Clint looked up and down the hall and wondered why no one had come out to see what the fuss was. Probably because they didn't want to get killed.

He left the body where it was and went back inside to get dressed.

TWENTY-SEVEN

Clint got dressed, strapped on his gun, and went looking for a vacant hotel room. He did this by knocking on doors until no one answered. When he found such a room he forced the door and went inside. He doubted that any rooms would be rented out late at night, so he figured he was safe until morning. He lay down on the bed fully clothed with his gun in his hand. Sometime during the night he heard some men in the hall grunting as if they were carrying something. He waited a few moments, then looked and saw that the body had been removed. By now, he thought, Sheriff Chadwick knew that his plan had failed. He might think that Clint had left town, but a check of the livery would dispel that theory. The lawman wouldn't find him unless he did a room by room search of the hotel.

Clint went back into the room and prepared it so

he could sleep. There was no window, so all he had to do was push the dresser in front of the door. If someone tried to kick the door in, all they'd be able to do was wake him up.

He lay back down on the bed, still fully dressed and still holding his gun, but this time he allowed himself to fall asleep.

He woke at first light. Even without a window he knew instinctively that the sun was up. He collected his gear, left the room, and found the back door of the hotel. He went out that way, figuring that the front was being watched. Using alleys he made his way to the saloon and found the back door there. He forced it and went inside. He didn't know that Fred lived above the saloon, but he was hoping that he did. He remembered what the man had said about not telling customers where he lived, but Clint suspected that Fred was more than just a bartender at the saloon. If he owned the place, it made sense that he'd live above it.

Clint found a rear staircase and went up. He wondered if Denise had a room up here. She was probably so scared she wouldn't open her door for anyone.

There were four doors on the second floor, but finding Fred's room became easy when he heard the snoring. It was the sound a heavy man made when he was asleep.

Clint tried the doorknob and found the door unlocked. He opened the door as quietly as he could, entered, and closed it behind him. He waited for his eyes to adjust to the darkness of the room, then picked out Fred's form on the bed. He walked to it and tapped the man on the head. Instead of waking, the man swatted Clint, as if he were a fly. Clint tapped him on the head again, but elicited the same response. This time he slapped Fred on the head and the man sat up quickly, blinking.

"Hey! What?"

"Wake up, Fred."

The man looked up at him, but couldn't see him in the dark. There was a lamp on the nightstand and Clint lit it and turned it up bright.

"Oh! Hey!" Fred said, shielding his eyes.

"It's Clint Adams, Fred. Wakey, wakey."

Fred began to rub his eyes, then looked up at Clint, frightened.

"It *is* you."

"That's right, it's me."

"What do ya want? I didn't do nothin'. Didn't Denise come to your room?"

"Yes, she did, as a matter of fact," Clint said. "She tried to keep me busy while some fella broke into my room and tried to kill me."

"What? That bitch! I didn't send nobody—"

"She told me the sheriff made her do it."

"Well, then, it wasn't me, right? That Chadwick, he's a son of a bitch."

"I just want to get some things straight, Fred, so relax, okay?"

"Relax," Fred repeated. "Okay, I'm relaxed."

"You did send Denise over to me, right?"

"Right," the man said, "but just to deliver a message—and if anything else happened, that was supposed to be between the two of you."

"Okay. What was the message you sent her with?"

Fred repeated the message, roughly word for word.

"And you don't know who the rich man is?"

"No."

"Or the woman's name."

"N-no."

"Come on, Fred."

"What?"

"How could you know what you told me but not know any names?"

Fred looked around heedlessly, as if for a way out.

"A name, Fred," Clint said, "that's all I want."

"The woman's name was . . . Bianca."

"What was her last name?"

"I don't know."

"And the man who was keeping her?"

"You think he killed her?"

"Had her killed, Fred," Clint said, "and you believe it, too, don't you?"

Fred closed his eyes.

"This could get me killed."

"Not if I get to them first."

Fred covered his face with his hands, then dropped them to his lap. He was wearing a red-and-white striped nightshirt that children could have used as a tent.

"I don't know the man's name," he said, "honest, but I do know where he lives."

Clint figured he was going to have to settle for that.

"All right, Fred, where?"

"Omaha."

Why didn't that surprise Clint? He had a feeling all along he'd be heading back to Omaha.

"You ever hear the name Percy, Fred?" Clint asked. "Michael Percy?"

Fred looked nervous.

"I heard of him."

"Could that be the man?"

"C-could be. I don't know. There's other rich men in Omaha."

"Yeah, I guess there are, at that," Clint said.

After a few moments of silence Fred asked nervously, "Is that it?"

"Not quite yet, Fred."

Fred rolled his eyes, as if wondering, What next?

"I need to know where you saw Anne Archer."

"Your friend?"

"That's right."

"Well, I ain't sure, but—"

"Think, Fred."

"Gimme a chance," Fred said, then realized he'd spoken sharply to a man he was afraid of.

"All right, Fred. Take your time."

"Look," Fred said, "I don't go far from here, ya know? The general store, the hardware store sometimes. I must have seen her during one of those times. Real pretty woman with red hair and wearing a gun. You can't miss her, ya know?"

"I know."

"Yeah, yeah, you would," Fred said. "Three blocks."

"What about three blocks?"

"I must have seen her within three blocks of here, either direction. Couldn't have been much further."

"How many hotels in that space?"

"Two."

"And a telegraph office?"

Fred thought a moment.

"Yeah, there is one."

"That's it, Fred," Clint said, after a moment. "You can go back to sleep now."

"W-what happened to Denise?"

"Nothing," Clint said. "She just got scared, that's all."

"Did you kill somebody else?"

"A man, Fred," Clint said, "just one man—but I may not be done yet."

Fred's eyes widened.

"No, I don't mean you, Fred," Clint said soothingly. "I have you to thank for giving me some information."

"Are you leaving town now?"

"I have to see one more person."

"The sheriff?"

"That's right."

"You gonna kill him?"

Clint walked to the door and turned before opening it.

"I guess that'll be up to him, Fred."

"Be careful," Fred said. "He always has somebody watching his back, even if you can't see him."

"Thanks, Fred," Clint said. "That information will be helpful."

TWENTY-EIGHT

Clint's first instinct was to go after the sheriff, but he thought twice about it. There was still some information he needed to find out about Anne Archer before he did that. He'd go after the man, all right, but that would have to come later.

Basically, he wanted to try to find out two things: where Anne had stayed while she was in Lincoln, and if she had gotten any telegrams. What he hoped to find was that she had gotten a telegram from her partners while she was here, and that would tell Clint where Sandy and Katy were. If Anne had gotten involved in the plans of a wealthy man who was not afraid to commit murder, then he'd likely have access to a lot of men. Already Clint had seen that he had one sheriff in his pocket and had been responsible for the death of another one.

He wondered how Sheriff Macy could have been so

111

wrong about Sheriff Chadwick, thinking that the man was a good lawman when he was, in fact, crooked.

Clint eased himself out the rear door of the saloon. Fred had told him there were two hotels and one telegraph office within three blocks. He meant to check them all out before he confronted Sheriff Chadwick. That would be just before he left town and headed back to Omaha, where he was sure Hank Barlowe would be waiting.

Everything he was going through—and would go through—would be worth it if he could find Anne Archer safe and sound in the end.

He found one of the hotels two blocks west of the saloon. It was then that he realized that his own hotel was the other one Fred was talking about. He'd check that one next.

He walked in and found the clerk dozing, his elbow on the desk, his chin in his hand. He rang the bell right next to the man's elbow and the clerk woke with a start.

"Need a room?" he asked, even before his eyes focused.

"No, I need to look at your register."

The man focused his eyes now and frowned from behind his thick glasses.

"If you don't want a room, why do you want to look at the register?"

"Just let me see it."

"I can't—" the man started, but then he saw the look in Clint's eyes. "Here." He pushed the book at him.

Clint opened it and turned to the last few pages, looking for Anne's room. It wasn't there.

"Son of a bitch," he said. If it turned out that she had stayed at the same hotel he was in, he was going to feel real dumb for not having checked the register there.

"Is there, uh, something wrong?" the man asked, hoping he wasn't about to become the object of Clint's anger.

"Forget it," Clint said. "Go back to sleep."

"Really?" The man looked surprised.

"Yeah, really," Clint said and walked out.

He walked into his own hotel carefully, just in case the sheriff or someone sent by him was in the lobby. He'd already determined that the street was clear. The clerk at the desk was not the one who had been on duty when he checked in.

"Can I help you?" the man asked. He was portly and balding, in his fifties.

"I'm already a guest, but I need to check the register to see if I wrote my correct address."

The man frowned.

"Your name?"

"Clint Adams."

The clerk opened the book and saw Clint's name it.

"You wrote—"

"Can I see it myself?"

"Well . . . all right."

The clerk pushed the register over to him. Clint reversed it and looked at his name, then looked at the other names on the page.

"Well, it looks right," he said, and turned to the page before.

"Hey—"

"Quiet!" he said coldly, and the man subsided.

There it was. Anne's name was the last one at the bottom of the page.

"Damn," he said, shaking his head. He looked at the clerk, who took an inadvertent step backward.

"Do you remember this woman? Anne Archer?"

"Uh—"

"A beautiful red-haired woman wearing a gun. Were you on duty when she checked in?"

"Oh, yes," the clerk said, "I remember her."

"Good. Did she get any telegrams while she was here?"

"Uh—"

"Come on, man, think. I'm not going to hurt you. Just answer the question."

"Yes, yes," the man said, "yes, the telegraph clerk did come over with a telegram for her, but she wasn't in."

"Did she ever pick it up?"

"I don't know . . . honestly."

"All right, relax," Clint said. "One last question."

"W-what is it?"

"Did you ever see Sheriff Chadwick with Miss Archer?" Clint asked.

"Uh . . . not here."

"What's that mean, not here?"

"Well, I did see him talking to her out on the street in front of the hotel."

"When?"

"The day she arrived."

"Do you have a newspaper from the day that woman was killed?"

"Well, I have some old newspapers—"

"Take a look."

The man started, then bent over and came out with a bunch of newspapers. He leafed through them and pulled out one.

"Here it is."

Clint took the paper and compared the date to the date Anne checked in. The woman had been killed the same night she'd arrived.

"When did she arrive?"

"Who?"

"The woman."

"W-which woman?" the man said. Then he hurriedly added, "You're confusing me."

Clint took a deep breath and got himself under control.

"The red-haired woman who registered in the hotel. What time of day did she arrive?"

"Uh, in the morning, she got here in the morning."

"And when did you see her with the sheriff?"

"Uh . . . soon after she arrived."

And the woman had been killed in the evening. The sheriff had probably picked Anne out almost immediately as a likely patsy.

The bastard.

"All right, thanks."

The clerk seemed surprised that Clint was just going to walk out, but he did. The man heaved a sigh of relief and wondered what he should do. Finally he simply cleared the newspapers off the desk.

TWENTY-NINE

He walked to the telegraph office, staying on the street this time and not taking to the alleys. He watched for the sheriff, or for anyone else who might be paying him special attention, but the early hour was working in his favor.

He entered the telegraph office, which appeared to have just opened.

"Be with you in a minute," said the visored key operator.

"I don't want to send a telegram."

The man looked at him.

"What then?"

"I've got some questions."

The key operator was a squat, powerfully built man who could have been fifty or sixty. He had a brush mustache that completely hid his upper lip, and he touched it now.

"I don't have time for questions. I've got to set up for the day."

"Make time."

"Now, mister," the man said, "you're taller than me, and you're a whole lot younger than me, but I wouldn't put my bet down too soon which of us would end up standing if we tangle. That is, unless you figure to use that gun on me."

Clint stared at the man and had to admire his spunk.

"You called my bluff."

"Yeah, I guess I did."

"What's your name?"

"Wilford."

"Well, Wilford, I've got a problem that I hope you can help me with."

"Well, sir, that's what you should have said from the git go. I've got a pot of coffee goin' here. Would you like some?"

"Sure, why not? Thanks."

When Wilford came back with two cups of coffee, he saw Clint looking out the window.

"Avoidin' somebody?"

Clint looked at the older man and took one of the cups from him. He decided to be honest.

"The sheriff."

"At odds with him, are you?"

"It seems so."

"Over what? You can close that door if you want. I can open some late."

Clint closed the door.

"Why are you doing this?" he asked.

"I think maybe you've got an interesting story to tell, and this job is borin' as hell."

Clint told the man the story and ended with his theory that the sheriff had chosen Anne as a patsy as soon as she rode into town.

"That's a shame," Wilford said. "Pretty woman like that."

"Then you spoke to her?"

"Sure did. She wanted to send a telegram to a couple of friends of hers."

"And you sent it?"

"Sure did."

"Did a reply come?"

"It did, but I couldn't find her to give it to her."

"That's odd."

"What is?"

"Well, if her partners hadn't heard from her they would have come here."

"Well, now, there you got me."

"What do you mean?"

"Well, sir, I tried to find her with her reply, like I said. When I couldn't I just brought it back here."

"And?"

"The sheriff came in a little later and asked for it."

"He must have heard about it from the desk clerk at the hotel."

"Exactly right. He asked me for it and I gave it to him. After all, he is the law. I had no choice."

"Okay."

"He read it and drafted a reply right there and then, told me to send it."

"You had no choice."

"Thank you. I didn't like it, but I done it. Been waitin' for somebody like you to come along and right my wrong ever since."

"Well, I'm here."

"So you are. Just a second."

Wilford went behind his counter, scraped around back there for a few seconds, and then came back around and handed Clint two telegraph flimsies.

"Copies?" Clint asked.

"You betcha. The sheriff destroyed the originals after I sent 'em, but I fooled 'im and made copies."

Clint read both copies. The first one was from Sandy and Katy, asking Anne if she wanted them to meet her in Omaha or Lincoln. The reply drafted by Chadwick was short and to the point. It said no, that she'd contact them if she needed them.

"Was there another reply after this?" Clint asked.

"No, sir, just the two you have there."

"Wilford, do you remember where the reply came from?"

The man smiled—at least, Clint thought he was smiling beneath his mustache.

"I sure do."

THIRTY

Clint found a likely place to hide himself—an alley, naturally—so that he could keep an eye on the sheriff's office. He only wanted to enter if the man was alone.

Before leaving the telegraph office, he had sent a telegram to the address that Wilford had for Sandy Spillane and Katy Littlefeather. The telegram they had sent had both of their names on it. He then told Wilford to keep any reply that came in and he'd check back later for it.

He saw Chadwick arrive, unlock the door, and go inside. He waited to see if anyone would come out, or if anyone else would go in. When he was sure the sheriff was alone, he crossed the street and entered.

Chadwick was standing at a potbellied stove, making a pot of coffee. He had the pot in one hand and coffee grounds in the other when he turned and looked at Clint's gun.

"You have me at a disadvantage," he said.

"Put the grounds in the pot and the pot on the stove," Clint said. "Try to throw either of them my way and I'll kill you."

Chadwick stared at him.

"It might almost be worth a try."

"Go ahead, then," Clint said.

Chadwick seemed to consider it, then shook his head and decided it wasn't worth it, after all. He put the grounds in the pot and set the pot down.

"Now undo the gun belt and let it drop."

Chadwick tried to maintain a dignified front as he did what he was told.

"Walk away from it, over there by the wall."

He obeyed.

Clint walked to the gun belt and kicked it across the room.

"Now what?" Chadwick asked. "I am an officer of the law, you know. This could get you into a lot of trouble."

"Maybe I should just kill you, then."

For a moment Chadwick's front slipped.

"You wouldn't."

"Why not?"

"You're . . . not a killer."

"You framed a friend of mine for murder, put her on the run," Clint said. "Why shouldn't I kill you?"

"Now, look, none of that was my idea."

"It wasn't, huh? Tell me something, Sheriff. Who

really killed that woman? You?"

"I don't kill women, Adams."

"No, you just frame them for murder so they'll be executed."

"I told you, that wasn't my idea."

"That's bull. You picked her out as soon as she got to town."

"I meant it wasn't my idea to frame someone."

"But you picked her."

"It wasn't personal. She was a stranger in town, is all."

"Well, it's personal now."

Clint stared at Chadwick long enough for the man to start to squirm. He saw the lawman's eyes flick to his desk and guessed that there was a gun in one of the drawers.

"Wh-what are you going to do?"

"You're going to talk to me, Sheriff. Give me a name."

"You want to know who killed the woman?"

"I think I already know that."

Chadwick frowned.

"How could you?"

"I'm guessing Hank Barlowe."

Chadwick didn't respond, but Clint saw something flicker in his eyes.

"No, the name I want is the man you work for, Chadwick, the man who's got your badge in his pocket."

"I—I can't tell you that."

"Why not?"

"He'd have me killed."

"I'll kill you now if you don't tell me."

"No," Chadwick said, "you wouldn't."

"Yes, I would."

They matched stares and then Chadwick said, "Yes, you would."

"I'm glad you agree."

"You're not leaving me much choice."

"No, I'm not."

In a flash Clint knew he'd misunderstood the man's remark. Chadwick didn't mean that he had no choice but to talk. He meant he had no choice but to go for the gun in his drawer.

Which he did.

THIRTY-ONE

There was only one shot and Clint rushed to the window to look outside to see if anyone had heard it. He watched for several seconds, but there was no activity at all, so he locked the door and went back to the desk.

The sheriff had slumped forward over it and he left him there. He was upset that he'd had to kill the man. He was, even after all he'd done, a lawman, and Clint was not in the habit of shooting officers of the law.

He decided to go through the man's desk, hoping that there would be something there that would lead him to whoever Chadwick had been working for. The only rich man he knew of in Omaha was the one Macy had told him about, Michael Percy, but that didn't mean that he was the one. Still, if Barlowe worked for Percy it was a connection. After all, Barlowe had stalked him in Omaha and—judging from the reaction of Sheriff Chadwick—had probably killed the woman, Bianca. If Barlowe was involved, and he usually worked for Percy, then the chances were good that Percy was involved, also.

Clint had to shift Chadwick's body to go through the drawers on that side of the desk. He found the gun the man had been going for, but not much else. He had to give up. There was nothing left for him to do in Lincoln. If Anne Archer had found out who framed her she would have gone to Omaha. Once there, though, wouldn't she have tried to keep her appointment with him?

He had to go back to Omaha now and finish things there. First, though, he had to go back to the telegraph office and see if there was an answer from Sandy and Katy. After that he'd have to reclaim Duke and get out of town before the sheriff's body was found.

Before leaving the office he dragged the sheriff's body back into one of the cells, so that no one could see it by peering through a front window. He took the man's key from his pocket and went to the front door. He peered outside to make sure no one was around, then quickly stepped out and locked the door behind him. He started to walk casually down the street and dropped the key into a nearby horse trough.

When Clint reached the telegraph office and slipped inside, Wilford looked at him expectantly.

"There's something you should know," Clint said immediately and told the man what had happened.

"It sounds like self-defense," Wilford said.

"It was," Clint said, "but understand that I don't have time to stay behind and prove it."

The man frowned.

"Does this make me an accessory?"

Clint couldn't lie to him.

"At this point, it might."

Wilford rubbed his hand over the lower portion of his face.

"I guess you shouldn't have told me about it, then."

"I didn't want you to hear about the shooting later and think I ran away."

"But you are, aren't you?"

"No, I'm not."

"But you are going back to Omaha."

"Yes, but only to try and save my friend."

"And then what?"

"And then I'll come back here and clear this matter up," Clint said.

"Until then only you and I will know that you killed Sheriff Chadwick."

"That's right."

Clint could see that this disturbed the man.

"You could turn me in now, Wilford," Clint said. "I won't try to stop you."

"You'll come back?" he asked.

"I swear," Clint said. "When I've done what I have to do I'll come back."

"God go with you, then."

Clint smiled at the man, thanked him, and headed for Omaha.

THIRTY-TWO

Michael Percy stared across his desk at Hank Barlowe.

"He's not back yet," Percy said.

"He'll be back," Barlowe said with assurance.

"When?" Percy asked. "You should have gone after him."

"It didn't make any sense to go after him," Barlowe maintained, "not after what happened with the sheriff."

"That was a farce!" Percy said. "How could you do that?"

"He pushed me," Barlowe said simply.

"A man in your position shouldn't push so goddamned easily."

Barlowe just stared at Percy, who refused to fidget in his chair, even though he wanted to.

Michael Percy was a self-made man who had refused for years to be intimidated by anyone, let alone a common gunman. Even though he harbored a secret fear of Hank Barlowe, he'd never let the man see it.

Percy was a large man, in his early fifties, with a shock of gray going through his still black hair. He wore a three-piece suit and a freshly boiled white shirt every day that he spent in his office.

"Besides," Barlowe said, "it wouldn't be safe for me to go back to Lincoln . . . not after what happened there."

Percy made a face and executed a gesture of dismissal with his hand. What happened in Lincoln was of little consequence to him, except where it affected his personal life. The fact that he had Bianca Chapman killed was no more than a business decision, the discharge of an annoyance. Now he had only to take care of the small matters that came after.

"What about the Archer woman?"

Barlowe shook his head.

"No sign of her."

"That damned idiot Chadwick!" Percy swore. "Why couldn't he have taken care of her?"

Barlowe smiled.

"She was too much woman for him."

"Obviously," Percy said. "She is turning out to be too much woman for everyone."

Now Barlowe scowled.

"Not everyone."

Percy pointed a finger at him.

"If you want that bonus I promised you, you have

to take care of her *and* Adams."

"I know my job."

"Then do it."

"I might need help."

"You have Castle."

Barlowe's look now was one of contempt.

"Castle!" he said, as if it were a dirty word.

Percy sighed.

"All right, hire whatever help you need—but I want you to handle this personally, Barlowe. I need to know that it's done."

"You'll know."

Barlowe stood up and walked to the door.

"How do you know Adams will be back?" Percy asked. "How can you be so sure?"

Barlowe turned and said, "We have unfinished business, he and I."

"Like what?"

"He'll blame himself for what happened to Sheriff Macy. He'll want to settle with me. He'll be back."

Percy watched Barlowe leave, then sat back in his chair. Barlowe killing Sheriff Macy was bad luck. He probably wouldn't be able to use Barlowe anymore after this, and he wondered where he would find someone else who would be as useful. He also wondered idly who he would be able to use to get rid of Barlowe—that is, if the Gunsmith didn't kill him. Maybe they'd kill each other and solve both problems for him.

What were the chances of that happening? Everything Michael Percy had achieved over his lifetime had come hard. Why should this be any different?

THIRTY-THREE

Clint decided not to push Duke during the ride from Lincoln to Omaha. An hour or two wouldn't make a difference and it would still be dark when they got there. He needed the cover of darkness to enter Omaha because he knew Hank Barlowe would be there waiting for him.

He also hoped that Anne Archer would be there. If she was, she'd also have to be smart enough to stay under cover.

Before Clint had left Lincoln, Wilford had given him the reply he'd gotten from Sandy Spillane and Katy Littlefeather. They were in California, where they were waiting for Anne. According to their telegram she was planning to meet Clint in Omaha, and then meet them in San Francisco. As it stood, it would take them a while to get to Nebraska. Clint sent them another telegram telling them to stay put and he'd notify them when he found Anne. He didn't wait for an answer.

Clint could see the lights of Omaha up ahead. He circled for a while, because he wanted to come in near the hotel he had stayed in. He hoped that Barlowe would not expect him to come back to the same place. Not that he wanted to avoid Barlowe completely, but he did want to stay away from the man long enough to find Anne. Once that was done, he and Barlowe would settle up. Clint still felt completely responsible for what had happened to Sheriff Macy, and Barlowe was going to have to pay for that.

Finally he thought he had the right angle and directed Duke into town. He came upon a back alley where he dismounted. He walked Duke a short way, then decided to leave him behind while he found the hotel. He knew the big gelding would wait right there for him. There wasn't much chance of anyone finding him at this time of night, and even if someone did they'd never get the big horse to move.

"Wait," he said and moved away into the darkness.

Clint had miscalculated slightly, but at least he was in the right neighborhood. He had to make up several blocks, but he was able to do that on back alleys. Finally, when he came to the back of the hotel he was able to force the rear door and enter.

Once inside he went over his options. He could find a vacant room and stay in it as long as was possible—at least until the hotel rented it out. That would mean going door to door to find one, and what would he do if there weren't any rooms available?

His second option was to approach the clerk and find out if Anne Archer had ever arrived, asking for him. If not he could get his old room back and wait. Unfortunately, he'd be waiting not only for Anne Archer, but for Hank Barlowe, or whoever had replaced Sheriff Macy—possibly even Deputy Young and his men.

Clint decided to try to find out who the clerk on duty was. If it was Bob then maybe he could get the young man to go along with him.

He crept down a hallway he thought would lead him to the lobby. As it turned out, it led him to the kitchen, which at this hour of the morning was empty. The same went for the dining room. They wouldn't even be setting up for breakfast for another two or three hours.

He left the kitchen, crossed the empty dining room with the chairs on top of the tables until he got to the entrance. Peering out he saw that Bob, the more friendly of the clerks, was on the desk. He decided to simply approach him and see what happened.

He left the dining room and walked to the desk. Bob looked up as he heard footsteps and then looked surprised when he saw Clint.

"Jesus," he said, "I didn't hear you come in—wait a minute. You didn't come in the front way, did you?"

"No, I didn't, Bob."

"Where did you come from? I didn't even know you were back in town."

"Nobody knows," Clint said. "Nobody but you and me."

Bob's eyes widened.

"What makes me so lucky?"

"I came in the back way, Bob. I'm trying to avoid being seen."

"By who? The law?"

"The law, and Hank Barlowe, and anyone else who might be working for Michael Percy."

"Mr. Percy? What's he got to do with anything?"

"Barlowe works for him, doesn't he?"

"I don't know—I guess so—sometimes."

"Did anyone come looking for me while I was gone, Bob?" Clint asked.

"Like who? Barlowe?"

"Like anybody."

"Oh, you mean your friend, the lady with the gun?" Bob asked, suddenly catching on.

"That's right, my friend."

"No, she didn't come in."

"Who did? Come on, Bob, you're holding out on me."

"You know," Bob said, "it really ain't fair for you to ask me to help you, especially if Mr. Percy's involved."

"Why is that, Bob?"

"Because," Bob said, "Mr. Percy owns this hotel."

That surprised Clint.

"He owns the hotel?"

Bob nodded.

"Then that means . . ."

"That's right," Bob said, "he's also my uncle."

THIRTY-FOUR

A half hour later Clint and Bob were sitting in the dining room. Bob had gone into the kitchen and made a pot of coffee. They had taken the chairs down off one of the tables and were sitting so they could see the lobby and the front desk.

"So if he's your uncle," Clint asked, "why do you call him 'mister'?"

Bob shrugged.

"He insists."

"Why?"

"He likes it better than being called 'Uncle,' I guess. Besides, he doesn't really like me."

"Why do you have a job, then?"

"Because his sister was my mother—but I probably have the lowest paying job he could have given me. He owns lots of businesses in Omaha, and there were lots of other jobs he could've given me."

"Well, it looks like I've put you in a bad spot, Bob," Clint said.

"What do ya mean?"

"Well, you know I'm back in town, and since you're related to Percy you obviously don't want to help me. You know what that means, don't you?"

Bob swallowed and asked, "What?"

Clint looked right into his eyes and said, "I've got to kill you."

Bob just stared back at Clint, hardly breathing. In fact, he wasn't breathing, he was holding his breath. Clint waited until he started to turn blue.

"Relax, Bob," Clint said, "I'm kidding."

Bob let his breath out and said, "You shouldn't kid like that, Mr. Adams. Jesus, I like to had a heart attack."

"What's it going to be, Bob?"

"What? Oh, you mean will I help you? Well, sure. I mean, I don't even like my uncle."

"Well, good . . . I mean, good that you're going to help me. I'm, uh, sorry you don't like your uncle."

"You're, uh, not gonna kill him or anything like that, are you?"

"Why would I kill him, Bob?"

"Well . . . I mean, if he was gonna try to kill you I could understand it, but you, uh, ain't just gonna kill him . . . are you?"

"No, Bob," Clint said, "I'm not just going to kill him."

"And Barlowe?"

"Barlowe killed the sheriff," Clint said. "He's got to pay."

"You're gonna kill him?"

"Or have him arrested. Has Sheriff Macy been replaced yet?"

Bob nodded.

"The deputy, Young, he took over until the town council can find a regular replacement."

"Has he been here looking for me?"

"Just once."

"He might come back."

"What do I tell him?"

"Tell him that you haven't seen me since the day the sheriff was shot."

"Uh, okay."

"Are there any empty rooms in the hotel, Bob?"

"Sure, plenty."

"Good, I'll need one."

"Okay."

"This is very important."

"What is?"

"Don't rent out the room I'm using."

"Oh, sure, I won't."

"And tell the other clerks the same thing."

"What do I tell them is the reason?"

"You're the boss's nephew," Clint said. "You don't have to give them a reason."

"Oh," Bob said, "right."

"I'm going to get my horse out of sight before the sun comes up," Clint said, rising. "Remember, Bob, you haven't seen me."

"No, sir," Bob said, "I surely haven't."

"Okay, then," Clint said, "give me a room key and get back behind the desk."

THIRTY-FIVE

Clint tucked Duke behind the hotel. Later on he'd go and have the same talk with Fingers that he'd had with Bob. Hopefully the old man would be as co-operative as the hotel clerk and Wilford, the Lincoln telegraph clerk, had been. Even Fred, the bartender from Lincoln, had helped. God, if only someone that helpful had seen Anne Archer in the past few days. . . .

Clint apologized to Duke for leaving him standing in the alley, promised to get him into the stable as soon as possible, and went back into the hotel through the rear door. Bob had given him the key to room ten, which was in front of the hotel. Clint didn't mind having a room with a window that overlooked the street because no one knew he was there. Also, he'd have a clear view of the street.

Even though he didn't think Bob would turn him

in, he blocked the door with a chair and set the pitcher and bowl from the dresser on the windowsill so no one could sneak up on him. He wanted to get a couple of hours' sleep before he walked Duke over to the livery to talk to Fingers. The old man had taken a shine to Duke, and Clint was almost certain he would take the big horse in without much of a fuss.

He took off his boots and stretched out on the bed, hands clasped behind his head. His gun belt was hanging on a nearby chair, but the gun was on the bed next to him. He closed his eyes and dozed off, sleeping lightly. . . .

As the sun started to come up, Hank Barlowe stepped out of the boardinghouse he was staying in and saw two men waiting for him.

"Mornin', Hank," Dan Connick said.

"Dan."

The other man, Walt Garrett, simply nodded. Both men had ridden over from Council Bluffs at Barlowe's behest by telegram the day before. They had worked with him previously.

"What we got?" Connick asked.

"You boys are gonna thank me for this," Barlowe said. "I'm lettin' you in on—"

"Uh-oh," Walt Garrett said.

"You reelin' us in again, Hank?" Connick asked.

"What are you talkin' about?"

"Last time you told us we was lucky we almost got killed," Connick pointed out. Garrett agreed with an enthusiastic nod.

"Last time you fellas made a ton of money, as I recall."

"Almost didn't live to spend it," Connick said.

"That was different," Barlowe said.

"How?" Connick asked.

"We didn't know what we were up against then."

"And we do now?"

"Yes."

"What?" Connick asked.

"Clint Adams."

"Clint . . ." Connick said.

". . . Adams?" Garrett said.

"That's right."

"Are you crazy?" Connick asked.

"The Gunsmith," Garrett said. "Clint Adams is the goddamned Gunsmith."

"And you want us to go up against him?" Connick asked.

"No."

Connick and Garrett exchanged a glance.

"No?" Connick asked.

"No."

"Then . . . what?"

"A woman."

"What?" Garrett asked.

"You want us to kill a woman?" Connick asked.

"That's right."

"What for?" Garrett asked.

"For a lot of money," Barlowe said, "that's what."

"What about the Gunsmith?" Connick asked.

"He's mine," Barlowe said. "I don't even want you two near him."

Again the other two men exchanged a glance.

"You think you can take the Gunsmith?" It didn't matter which of them asked it, they both wanted to know.

"If I didn't," Barlowe said, "none of us would be here."

"What about this woman?" Connick asked, after a few moments of silence had passed among them.

"She's a bounty hunter."

"Who is she here for?" Garrett asked.

"That doesn't matter," Barlowe said. "We're being paid to get rid of her."

"How much?" Connick asked.

Barlowe told them and both men looked surprised.

"That much?" Connick asked.

"For a woman?" Garrett said.

"That's right," Barlowe said, "for a woman."

"Boy," Connick said, "that makes me wonder what you're gettin' for Adams."

Barlowe just gave Connick a hard stare in reply.

"Hey," the man said, backing off, "I just said I was wonderin'."

"Well, stop wonderin'," Barlowe said. "I'm gonna give you a description of the woman. Go and find her and do it. Understand?"

"We understand," Connick said. "Don't we, Walt? Walt?"

"Huh?" Walt Garrett had been wondering if the money offered was enough for him to kill a woman for the first time. "Oh, right, we understand."

After all, money was money.

THIRTY-SIX

When Connick and Garrett left Barlowe, Connick asked his partner what was wrong with him.

"Nothin'," Garrett said.

"Somethin's botherin' you," Connick said. "Is it because we have to kill a woman?"

"We don't *have* to do nothin' we don't want to do, Dan," Garrett said.

Connick put his hand on Garrett's arm to stop him.

"You ain't never killed a woman before, have you, Walt?"

"Well . . . no." Defiantly he then asked, "Have you?"

"Well . . . no. But how different can it be from killin' a man?"

"I don't know."

"And the money's good."

"I know that."

141

"Then what's the problem?"

Garrett shrugged.

"I guess there ain't one."

"Good," Connick said, "then let's find this gal and take care of business."

"Okay."

They started walking again and after a few minutes Garrett said, "She sure sounds pretty, though. . . . "

Clint awoke with a start, even though he'd been sleeping very lightly. He looked around and saw the light coming in through the window. He got up, walked to the window, and studied the street in front of the hotel. He hadn't overslept. The street was deserted, and the light that was coming in through the window was brand-new.

He pulled on his boots, strapped on his gun, and quit the room. He had to get Duke to the livery before someone saw him.

Just seconds after Clint moved away from the window, Hank Barlowe came into view, walking purposefully toward the sheriff's office. He had to get things straight with acting sheriff Young, find out whether he was going to help or simply stay out of the way. That was important. He'd already killed one lawman, he didn't want to take a chance on killing another one.

Clint walked Duke to the livery. In order to get there he had to come around to the main street and

approach the livery from the front. He looked both
ways before coming out of the alley with the big gelding. He had no idea that he had just missed Barlowe
going into the sheriff's office.

He got to the livery as the old man, Fingers, was
opening the door.

"Are you back?" Fingers asked.

"I'm back."

"Want me to take care of the big fella for ya?"

"That's right, Fingers."

"What else?"

"What do you mean?"

"You want somethin' else from me," Fingers said.

"How do you know?"

The old man's face spread into a smile, causing
even more wrinkles than he already had.

"I can smell it, young fella," he said. "Come on
now, tell Uncle Fingers what's goin' on."

"I need to lay low for as long as possible, Fingers,"
Clint said.

"From the law?"

"From the law . . . from Hank Barlowe and Michael Percy, as well."

Fingers peered at Clint and asked, "You goin' up
agin Percy?"

"I'm not sure."

"But you are goin' up agin Barlowe?"

"Looks like it."

"Well, same thing, then," Fingers said. "Barlowe
works for Percy."

"I heard that he sometimes works for him."

"More times than not," Fingers said.

"What do you say?" Clint asked. "Is it going to be a problem for you if the law comes looking?"

"Law," Fingers said, then snorted. "Ain't no law now with Macy dead. Say, this got anythin' to do with that?"

"It does."

Fingers raised his eyebrows then.

"Barlowe killed him, ain't that it?"

"That's it."

"Did you tell the deputy?"

"I did."

"Well, sure," Fingers said, catching on, "he won't do nothin' about it. Not without witnesses."

"There were witnesses."

"But they won't talk, huh?"

"That's right."

"All right, young fella," Fingers said, taking Duke's reins from Clint. "You do what you gotta do and I'll take care of the big fella for ya."

"Thanks, Fingers."

"You get it done and come back, ya hear?"

"I hear."

"Come on, Duke," Fingers said, and continued talking in a low voice to the horse while he walked him inside.

THIRTY-SEVEN

"So what's it gonna be, Deputy?" Barlowe asked.

"Sheriff," Young said. "I'm sheriff now."

"For a little while, is all," Barlowe said. "As soon as they find somebody else they like, you'll be out on your ear. He probably won't even keep you on as a deputy, whoever they hire."

"Why not?"

"New sheriffs like to hire their own men, you know. You'll be out of a job."

Young stared at Barlowe, probably trying to figure out if he was right or not.

"Stay off the streets for a few days, Dep—I mean, Sheriff."

"Look, Barlowe," Young said, "whatever happens later, I'm the sheriff now. I can't just let you—"

"You gonna stop me . . . Sheriff?" Barlowe asked, cutting the man off.

Young just stared.

"You gonna stand up to me?"

Young started shifting from foot to foot.

"I'm just saying—"

"*I'm* just saying stay off the streets and you'll stay a lawman a little longer."

Barlowe left the new sheriff standing there with only his humiliation to keep him company.

But at least he was alive.

Outside Barlowe stood and took a deep breath. There was dampness in the air, but that could go on for some time before it actually rained.

He stepped down into the street and started across. At least now he wouldn't have to worry about some badge carrier getting in the way. As for the woman, Connick and Garrett would take care of her, leaving him clear to handle Clint Adams.

He was still dead sure that Adams would be back from Lincoln. Even if he wasn't, it wasn't likely that he'd leave the area without learning what happened to his girlfriend. Eventually, if he had to, he'd just go to Lincoln and get him. Either way, the man was his.

Barlowe reached the other side of the street and stopped. What would he do if he were Clint Adams? If he was back in Omaha he sure wouldn't want anyone to know, but he'd still need a place to stay, and a place for his horse.

He turned left and started walking toward the hotel and, beyond that, the livery.

THIRTY-EIGHT

Clint came away from the livery and immediately spotted Hank Barlowe crossing the street. The man hadn't looked his way, so he ducked into the livery again.

"What's the matter?" Fingers asked.

"Hank Barlowe."

"Is he headed this way?"

"I don't know."

Fingers came up behind Clint as he peeked out and saw Barlowe start walking toward them.

"Coming here or going to the hotel," Clint said. "One of the two, I guess."

"He ain't gonna find out anything here," Fingers said. "What about the hotel?"

"I don't know," Clint said.

"Bob there?"

"Yes."

"He's Percy's nephew, you know."

"I know."

"No tellin' what he'll do."

Clint looked at Fingers.

"I guess not. Look, if he comes in here, you tell him what you know."

"I thought—"

"He's going to see Duke, anyway," Clint said. "You can't very well hide him."

Fingers looked over at the big gelding and said, "That's for sure."

"So you tell him, you hear. I don't want to be responsible for any more deaths."

"You want a back way out?" Fingers asked.

"Yes."

Fingers frowned.

"You ain't afraid of him," the old man said. "I can see that."

"No, I'm not."

"Then why are you doin' this?"

"I've got other things to do first, Fingers."

Fingers nodded, satisfied with Clint's vague reply. "You better go out the back before Barlowe shows up," he said. "I'll stall him."

"Stall him, but don't put yourself at risk. All right?"

"Sure."

"I mean it, Fingers."

"I hear you. Now you go!"

Fingers led Clint to the back and unlocked a small door that Clint had to duck through to get out. It closed behind him and he heard the lock snap back into place.

As he stood there behind the livery, he realized he didn't have any idea where to go from there. He decided then to go back to the hotel, enter through the back again, and see what was going on.

THIRTY-NINE

Clint crept down a different hallway, now that he knew the other one led to the kitchen. This one led where he hoped it would, right behind the front desk. Barlowe was there talking to Bob. Apparently he'd gone first to the hotel.

"Bob, I could go right to your uncle and tell him that you know somethin' you're not tellin' me," the man said.

"Look, Mr. Barlowe—"

"Or I could just hurt you until you tell me."

Clint couldn't see Bob, but he could imagine the look on the man's face. To his credit Bob had not yet told Barlowe that Clint was in town, but Clint didn't expect him to hold out much longer.

"Or should I just kill you?"

"If I tell you . . . *he'll* kill me!" Bob complained. "It's not fair!"

"Tell you what, Bob," Barlowe said, and Clint heard the hammer being drawn back on a gun, "why don't you just decide if you want to die now or later, huh?"

"Jesus . . ." Clint heard Bob mutter. Go ahead, he thought, tell him.

"He's back in town," he finally heard the clerk say miserably.

"When?"

"This morning."

"Where is he?"

"I gave him room ten."

Clint heard pages being turned and then Barlowe said, "He's not in the book."

"He didn't sign in," Bob said. "I just gave him an empty room."

"And is he in it now?"

"I—I don't know."

"I'm gonna check, Bob," Barlowe said, "and if you're lying to me—"

"I'm not. I swear!"

"Just wait here until I come back."

Clint heard footsteps across the floor and then on the stairs. He slipped through the curtained doorway behind the desk, scaring Bob half to death.

"Jesus, you been there the whole time?"

"I have."

"Then you know I had to tell him—"

"Forget it, Bob. I know that. Tell me quickly where your uncle lives."

"He'd be in his office now."

"Quick then," Clint said, "directions to both."

Bob gave him the directions to the home and office of his uncle.

"What do I tell Barlowe when he comes down?"

"Nothing," Clint said. "He'll know I was in the room and that you told him the truth. If you feel your life is threatened, then tell him I was just here. Don't get yourself killed, all right?"

"I—I'll try not to tell."

"Do what's right for yourself, Bob. That's what I'm doing."

Clint turned and went out the front door.

Upstairs Hank Barlowe kicked in the door to room ten and went in with his gun drawn. Clint's saddlebags were on the floor, and the bed was rumpled. It looked to him like Bob was telling the truth. Adams had been there, but now was not.

Where would he go?

Barlowe turned and left the room, went back down to the lobby.

"You were tellin' the truth, Bob," Barlowe said. "That's good. Where's his horse?"

"The livery, I guess."

"If he comes back, don't give him a room. Understand? For your own good, don't help him."

"I understand."

"Good. There won't be any need for me to tell your uncle about this, then."

Bob nodded. He didn't care if Barlowe told his uncle or not. When Barlowe went out the door, he was leaving, too.

To hell with all of them.

FORTY

Michael Percy was not at home, nor was he at his office. It had not taken him long to replace Bianca Chapman as his mistress. Delores Mattes had been on the fringes for a few months, tossing hot looks his way. He knew she was waiting her turn, just as he knew she would get it. Now that she had, she was making the most of it.

She was busy between his legs now, nuzzling him, licking the length of his rigid penis and then taking it deeply into her mouth. When Bianca did that she had a habit of closing her eyes, but this hot little bitch stared right up at him even while riding him with her mouth. He found the look in her eyes to be quite exciting. Even as he swelled and then roared as he ejaculated she never took her eyes off him, accommodating every drop expertly. He wondered idly if the woman had ever been a whore. She was in her thirties—just about twenty years younger than he was—so who knew what she had done to survive up to this point. At the moment she owned and operated the ice cream store in a building she rented from him. He found it deliciously ironic that less than an hour ago she had been out front serving ice cream to children, and now she was in the back of the store with him, naked, sucking him dry.

When she released him from her mouth, she settled back on her haunches and continued to stare up at him. She had long dark hair that she usually wore up, but when she was with him she let it down around her shoulders. She was not a tall woman, but neither was she short. It was her large breasts and wide hips that made her look shorter than she was. Dressed, they almost made her appear chunky, but naked her curves were opulent. In this way she was the opposite of Bianca, who had been tall and sleek, small-breasted with almost no buttocks. One of the things Percy liked about Delores was that she had an ass.

"How about a cup of tea?" he asked.

"I'll bring it to you," she said, "and then I have to check on the store."

"Fine," he said.

He was sitting in an overstuffed armchair that she had taken into the back of the store for him. He stayed naked, a stocky man in his fifties who remained robust. In spite of the fact that he had been keeping a mistress for most of the twenty-eight years he and his wife, Margo, had been married, he still had sex with his wife three or four times a week. He loved her, and all of his mistresses knew he would never leave her. Why then had Bianca started to think otherwise? Why did she want to start trouble? No, when she began insisting that he spend more of his time with her, and then all of his time with her, he knew it was time for her to go away . . . permanently.

First he sent her to Lincoln, telling her that he would join her there in a few days. Then he sent Barlowe after her, to kill her. It was Chadwick's job to find someone to pin the murder on, and he chose the female bounty hunter. She had escaped from Chadwick, however, and ever since then Percy had been waiting for her to show up in Omaha. Instead, Clint Adams showed up, supposedly to meet with her. When the Gunsmith arrived, things got complicated. He had to be taken care of before the woman could talk to him.

"Here's your tea, dear," Delores said.

"Thank you, my dear."

She had dressed, once again donning the long brown skirt and white blouse she usually wore in her store. Her hair had also been pinned back up so that not a hair was out of place.

"I'll be back soon."

"No rush," he said. "I'm going to finish my tea and then go back to the office."

"Will I see you later?"

He frowned.

"I don't know, Delores. We'll have to wait and see."

She sensed his annoyance and apologized.

"I didn't mean to make demands . . ."

"It's all right," he said, extending a hand. She took it in both of hers and kissed it. "Go on, go to work. I'll see you when I can."

When she left the room, he sipped the tea. She had put in the right amount of sugar, four lumps. He sat there and patiently drank the hot liquid, then set the cup aside and got dressed.

The whole thing had been going on too long. The woman was staying so well hidden that even her friend, Clint Adams, couldn't find her. She had to be somewhere in Omaha, though. She wouldn't stay in Lincoln. Chadwick had bungled further by allowing her to overhear a conversation that would certainly lead her to Omaha looking for the man who had tried to frame her.

Where was she, though? And where was Adams now? Hank Barlowe had always been reliable up till now. More and more he was thinking that it was time to send Barlowe away the way he had sent Bianca away.

It was time to go back to his office. His life was an orderly one. He was in his office at certain hours of the day and at home at certain hours. The time he allotted for his mistress was known only to him. Delores may have thought he was going to see her again today, but he was not. She had already gotten her share of his time.

Now all he needed to keep his life in order were the deaths of the woman, Anne Archer, and Clint Adams, the Gunsmith.

Was that too much to ask?

FORTY-ONE

Because of the hour of the morning Clint tried Michael Percy's office first, but found it locked up tight. Apparently the man did not keep banker's hours. The sign on the door said simply: PERCY ENTERPRISES. Clint had no idea what the man's "enterprises" were, but they had obviously made him very rich.

Next he tried his house, and he decided to be bold about it. After all, Anne Archer's life could very well be hanging in the balance.

The house was two stories with two columns in the front. It appeared to be a smaller version of a Southern mansion, and Clint wondered if Percy had had it built special.

When he knocked on the door, it was answered by a handsome, elegant woman in her early fifties. Her hair had once been jet black but was now streaked with gray. She had probably been a full-bodied woman most of her life, but now he could see that her hips and waist had thickened. The thrust of her bosom, however, was still full and firm.

"Yes?"

"Mrs. Percy?"

"That's right. Can I help you?"

"Is your husband home, ma'am?"

"Why, no, he isn't."

"I, uh, checked his office, but he isn't there yet."

He saw her jaw firm as she compressed her lips.

"Would you know where he is, ma'am?"

"Why do you want him?"

"It's just some . . . private business."

"Having to do with what?"

"I really don't want to say—"

"What is your name, sir?"

"Clint Adams."

"I find that name familiar. Are you a man of some . . . reputation?"

"I'm afraid that I am, ma'am."

"Please," she said, "stop calling me that."

"I'm sorry, Mrs. Percy."

She looked away and said, "That's not much better."

"I don't—"

Abruptly she stood aside and said, "Would you come in, please."

"Thank you."

He entered and followed her into a lavishly furnished living room.

"I am not going to offer you refreshments, Mr. Adams, since this is not a social call."

"I understand."

"I am able to place you now. You have a reputation as a gunman, don't you?"

"In some circles . . ."

"I am not here to judge you, Mr. Adams. In point of fact, you don't seem that kind of man."

"Thank you."

"Are you looking for my husband to harm him in any way?"

"I hope not."

"Then what . . ."

"I'm looking for a friend of mine who may be involved with your husband."

She arched one eyebrow and asked, "A woman?"

"Yes, but it's not what you think. I, uh, believe that my friend is a danger to him."

"Why?"

"Mrs. Percy—"

"Please call me Margo," she said, "and don't worry about shocking me. I know the worst things about my husband, Mr. Adams, and I've stayed with him all these years. I believe, however, that my patience has just about come to an end." She rubbed her hands together and added, "I probably should have left him ten years ago, when I was still young enough to find . . . someone . . ."

"You're a very attractive woman . . . Margo."

"Really? Do you really think so?"

"Yes."

She stared at him for a few moments, then asked, "Would you bed me?"

"Uh, Margo, I, uh . . ."

"Under the right circumstances," she added hastily, "would you take me to bed? Am I attractive enough for that—or do you also prefer the company of younger women?"

"To be truthful," he said, "I don't prefer the company of younger women. I find I much more enjoy being with experienced women."

She hugged herself then and looked away.

"I'm afraid I'd be a disappointment to you, then. You see, I've never been with any man other than my husband since we were married, and my experience before that was extremely limited."

"Mrs. Percy—uh, Margo—"

"I know," she said, cutting him off, "you didn't come here for this. You're looking for my husband."

"Yes."

"Well, Mr. Adams, you will most likely find my husband with his most recent mistress. Her name is Delores Mattes and she runs the ice cream shop."

Clint didn't realize how surprised he looked until she commented on it.

"Don't be surprised," she said. "I've known about most of my husband's mistresses over the years. His last one disappeared under mysterious circumstances—but you weren't here, then. You wouldn't know about that."

"You mean Bianca?"

Now it was her turn to look surprised.

"You have heard about that?"

"Yes."

She frowned.

"Is your friend involved in that?"

"The sheriff of Lincoln tried to frame her for the murder."

"The sheriff of—you mean Chadwick? He worked for my husband?"

"I know. Another man who works for your husband killed her. Hank Barlowe."

"Barlowe! You mean Michael had his own mistress murdered?"

"I believe so, and then he tried to have my friend framed for the crime."

"That bastard! When was he going to get tired enough of me to have me killed?"

Clint didn't think that would happen. He thought if Percy was going to have his wife killed, he would have done it by now. In his own warped way, Michael Percy probably loved his wife, which was why he stayed with her.

"If you don't find him with the Mattes bitch, try his office," she said. "He should be there."

He turned to go to the door, then turned back and said, "Thank you, Margo."

"Just go," she said, still hugging herself.

He didn't move.

"Go," she said again, "and do what you have to do."

He nodded, turned, and left.

FORTY-TWO

Barlowe decided that he didn't need to go to the livery stable. If Clint Adams was in town, he'd be looking for his girlfriend, or for Barlowe, or—depending on what he'd found out from Chadwick—he'd go looking for the man behind it all—Michael Percy.

Barlowe left the hotel and headed for Percy's office. He knew that the man would be with his new mistress, the ice cream lady, but he'd have to show up at the office sooner or later—and so would Clint Adams.

As Barlowe came out of the hotel and started across the street, Anne Archer spotted him from her hiding place in an alley. She'd been laying low in an abandoned barn for the past couple days, but now it was time for her to come out of hiding and finally face Michael Percy and Hank Barlowe. It had taken her these past few days to reconstruct the events that led up to Sheriff Chadwick trying to frame her for a woman's murder. Now that she had all the facts, it was time to make a move to close the whole matter out.

She had her hair tucked up under her hat and was wearing clothing three sizes too big for her in an attempt to hide her curves. So attired, she followed Hank Barlowe from a discreet distance.

Connick and Garrett were starting to think they were never going to find this woman.

"What if she's not even in town?" Garrett asked. He was still hoping they wouldn't find her so he wouldn't have to go through with killing a woman.

"If Barlowe says she's in town, then we better keep looking," Connick said.

They were a few yards from the livery when they saw Barlowe come out of the hotel.

"There he is," Garrett said. "Let's ask—"

"Wait. Who's that?"

They saw a figure come out of an alley and fall in behind Barlowe.

"Who cares?" Garrett said. "It's not the woman we're looking for."

"Look at the way that person is walking," Connick said. "That ain't no man."

"Well, it ain't the woman we're lookin' for either," Garrett said. "That woman's fat."

"Come on," Connick said.

"Where?"

"Just come on, will ya? I wanna keep up."

"Keep up with what . . ." Garrett muttered, but he quickened his pace.

Coming down the street from the direction of the Percy house, the first thing Clint saw was the ice cream shop, and not Percy's office. They were both on the same street, but he didn't know which one he would come to first.

He looked inside the shop and saw a woman behind the counter, serving ice cream to an older woman and a child. He entered and held the door for the woman and child to leave. As he closed it he noticed the OPEN sign on it, with CLOSED on the reverse side.

"Can I help you?" the woman asked.

"I'm looking for Michael Percy."

The woman's handsome face suddenly closed up as tight as a fist.

"Why would Mr. Percy be here?"

"Are you Delores Mattes?"

The woman hesitated, then said, "Yes."

"Margo Percy told me I'd find her husband here."

"Margo—you mean, she kn—I mean, I—I don't know what you mean."

"You're blushing, Miss Mattes."

Her hand flew to her face, and then she started to cry silently.

"How did she know?"

"Oh, I got the feeling that Percy doesn't hide his

affairs from her very well. She said she knew about all of them from the day they got married."

"I can't believe—"

"Is he here, Miss Mattes?"

"Uh, no, no, he's not. H-he left here just a little while ago to go to his office."

"I see. Well, thanks."

He went to the door, opened it, and then stopped and looked at her again. She had a stunned look on her face, and her hands were still framing her cheeks.

"If I were you, Miss Mattes, I'd be very careful."

She looked at him and said, "Of what?"

"Well, for starters, of what happened to Michael Percy's last mistress, Bianca."

"Bianca Chapman? She left town."

"And went to Lincoln," Clint said. "Check the Lincoln newspapers of the past week. I think you'll find them very enlightening."

With that he went to the door. Before leaving, though, he turned her OPEN sign around so that it now said CLOSED. He thought she'd need some time to collect her thoughts.

FORTY-THREE

Michael Percy had been in his office only a half hour when Hank Barlowe walked in.

"What are you doing here? I thought you were looking for Adams."

"There's been a change in plans," Barlowe said.

"What are you talking about?"

Barlowe hooked a chair with his foot, pulled it over so he could sit directly across from Percy.

"We're gonna wait for Adams to find us."

"Here?" Percy asked incredulously.

"That's right."

"What makes you think he'll come looking for me?"

"Because it's what I would do."

"And what makes you think he even knows about me?" Percy demanded.

"Have you heard from Sheriff Chadwick in Lincoln lately?"

"Well . . . no."

"Believe me," Barlowe said, "Clint Adams left Lincoln with your name, or with a trail to your name. As of now, he knows who you are."

"You can't be sure of that."

Barlowe folded his hands across his belly and said, "It's my job to be sure."

Percy stared at Barlowe, not at all certain this was the right thing to do.

"Why here, Barlowe?"

"Because," Barlowe said, "this is where you are, and you're the man he wants."

"Remember," Percy said, "you killed Bianca, and Sheriff Macy."

"While working for you."

"I never told you to kill the sheriff."

Barlowe was about to reply, then stopped and took a deep breath.

"That's water under the bridge, Michael."

Percy started, for that was the first time Barlowe had ever called him by his first name. Now he was sure that Barlowe's usefulness had come to an end.

"Let's get Clint Adams and his bounty hunter girlfriend taken care of, and then maybe we can argue with each other."

"I don't argue with the help, Barlowe," Percy said. in an attempt to take back control of the situation.

Barlowe simply smiled at him and said, "We'll see."

FORTY-FOUR

When Anne Archer reached the building where
Michael Percy had his office, she was undecided
what to do. At the moment she knew that Barlowe was inside. If Percy was there, too, then
she'd have to deal with both of them. She already knew that Barlowe was a killer. She'd gotten that much from Chadwick when the lawman
was in a talkative mood. What she didn't know
was what kind of a man Percy was. Could he
handle himself, or did he hire others to do all
his fighting for him? She was probably better off
finding Clint and going up against Barlowe and
Percy together.

She was still trying to decide what to do when she
sensed someone behind her. She turned and saw two
men staring at her. Both wore guns and looked like
hard cases.

"See?" Connick said to Garrett. "Look at her face. That's her, man."

"What do you boys want?" Anne asked.

"We want you, ma'am," Connick said.

"You don't want me," she said.

"Why not?"

"You don't want to die, do you?"

Connick smirked, but Garrett wasn't so sure about this.

"Connick—" he said.

"Can't back down now, Garrett," Connick said.

"You want to back down, Garrett?" Anne asked, seizing the opportunity to address the man by name.

"Maybe she ain't the right one, Connick," Garrett said.

"Take off your hat, lady."

Anne was tired of hiding, tired of running from lowlifes. She removed the hat and dropped it on the ground while shaking out her red hair. It was long, not quite to her shoulders, a dark red rather than something fiery.

"That's her, all right."

Anne also discarded the oversized jacket she was wearing to hide her gun. Now she stood before them in a man's shirt and pants, both of which were so big she looked almost comical.

"Look, my quarrel is not with you two," she said. "It's with Barlowe and Percy. Why not let them fight their own battles?"

"We're being paid, dearie," Connick said, "and paid real well."

"I think you're in trouble, mister," she said to him.

"What do ya mean?" Connick asked, with a frown.

"Look at your friend. His heart isn't in this."

Connick took a quick glance sideways at Garrett, who was licking his lips and flexing the fingers of his gun hand.

"Garrett?"

The man said nothing, and for a moment Anne thought she had them. She was sure that if the second man, Garrett, backed down, the first would, as well, rather than face her alone.

"Come on, Garrett!" Connick said, and the man seemed to start.

"I-I'm with ya, Connick."

"All right, then," Connick said. He looked at Anne and asked, "Where do you want to do this? Here or out in the street?"

"Here's as good a place as any," she said, and surprised them as she drew her gun first.

When Clint came within sight of Michael Percy's office, he saw the two men bracing a lone figure. He didn't recognize the single person until she removed her hat and he saw her red hair.

"Jesus," he said to himself, "Anne."

She dropped her jacket to the ground and he started running, because he could sense what was about to happen. He also knew that he was going to get there too late.

He was about to shout when he saw Anne draw her gun. She fired once, then moved quickly to her left—as he had once advised her to do when facing more than one man—dropped to one knee and fired again. The two men staggered. One managed to get off a shot, but it struck the door which she had been standing in front of until she moved just seconds before.

By the time Clint reached the scene, both men were lying on their backs in the street. He stood over them and looked down. One of them was still alive, his eyes fluttering.

"She d-drew first," he said.

"Why not?" Clint asked.

"N-not . . . f-fair . . ." the man said.

Clint shook his head.

"How did you manage to stay alive this long with thinking like that?" he asked, but the man couldn't hear him.

He started toward Anne Archer, then stopped and looked up. Standing at a window were two men. One was Barlowe. The other, he assumed, was Michael Percy. He stared at them both for a few moments, then looked away and started toward Anne.

"I see you took my advice about moving," he said.

She grinned at him while reloading.

"I always take your advice, Clint."

"Well, now that you're done here," he said, looking back at the two men, "maybe you can tell me why you stood me up at the hotel?"

FORTY-FIVE

At the sound of the first shot both Percy and Barlowe sat up straight in their chairs. When the second shot came they were moving for the window. By the time the third shot struck the door downstairs, they were looking out. They watched as two men staggered back into the street and then fell.

"Jesus," Percy said. "Your men?"

"Yes," Barlowe said tightly.

"Who—" Percy started, but then stopped when he saw a man run over to the two fallen men.

"Adams!" Barlowe said.

"But . . . he didn't shoot them."

"No."

"Then who?"

Barlowe looked at Percy.

"The woman."

At that moment both men gazed out the window

again and Clint Adams looked up at them. Percy felt rooted to the spot while Clint's eyes burned into him.

Barlowe, on the other hand, experienced a quickening of his heartbeat. His throat went dry, but that was okay. That had never meant fear to him.

Clint looked away then and walked out of sight.

"Where are they?" Percy asked, almost in a panic.

"Out of sight," Barlowe said. "They'll be coming up here real soon."

Percy turned to face him.

"What do we do?"

"Do you have a gun?"

"I-in my desk."

Barlowe took a look and came out with an old Navy Colt.

"Jesus. Where did you get this?" He didn't wait for an answer. He checked the gun's action and saw that it would fire. He thrust it into Percy's hand.

"Sit at your desk and keep your hands out of sight. They might not suspect that you have a gun."

"Wha—"

"Do it!"

Percy sat down shakily behind his desk and, holding the gun in his right hand, settled both hands out of sight in his lap.

"We'll wait for them to come up here," Barlowe said. "As soon as I draw my gun, you shoot the woman."

"What?"

"You take the woman," Barlowe said, "and I'll take Adams."

Percy stared at him for a few seconds and then said, "Shoot the woman?"

"Come on, Michael!" Barlowe snapped. "You hired me to kill a woman for you. You mean to tell me you can't kill one yourself?"

"That's what I hired you for!"

Barlowe turned and backhanded Percy across the face. The man sat there stunned and did not react.

"I'm not gonna get killed because you can't shoot a woman, Percy. Do you want to die?"

"N-no."

"Then when I draw on Adams," Barlowe said, very slowly and carefully, "you shoot the woman. Can you understand that?"

"I u-understand."

"Good," Barlowe said. He stood next to Percy and stared at the door. "Now we wait."

Clint gave Anne a big hug after she had finished reloading her gun and had holstered it. The shots had to have been heard, but no one had come out to see what was happening. There were, however, people watching from their windows.

"I'm sure glad to see you finally," Anne said.

"You okay?" he asked.

"Been laying low," she told him.

"I know all about it."

He took a moment to look at her. She was a beautiful woman, full, lush lips, lovely eyes with heavy eyebrows the color of her hair.

"Your hair's longer."

She touched it.

"Do you like it?"

"Very much," he said, "I like it *very* much."

She smiled at the compliment.

He stared at her for a moment and then said, "Well, are you ready?"

She nodded and said, "I'm ready. Let's finish it."

He reached past her to open the door, then stopped and asked, "What was the original reason you asked me to meet you here?"

"Oh, that," she said. "Sandy, Katy, and I had just made a lot of money for bringing in the Kadisson brothers. I just wanted you to help me spend some of it."

"Well," he said, "I guess we can do that when we're done here."

He reached past her then and opened the door.

FORTY-SIX

The stairway leading up to the second floor was wide enough for them to ascend abreast. They climbed silently, weapons drawn.

At the top of the stairs they looked around until they saw the door that had PERCY ENTERPRISES on it.

"I'll take Barlowe," Clint told her. "You take Percy."

She didn't argue. She'd heard a lot of stories about Barlowe since she got to Lincoln. He was younger than Clint, but was he faster?

That remained to be seen.

Michael Percy kept his eyes on the door, and when the doorknob started to turn he thought he was going to vomit. He had never been so frightened in his life. This was everyone else's fault, not his. It was Bianca's fault for starting all the trouble in the first place.

It was Sheriff Chadwick's fault for picking this woman to try to frame for Bianca's murder. And it was Barlowe's fault for not having already killed the woman and Clint Adams.

Everyone else had gotten him into this situation, but he was going to have to get himself out.

Clint turned the doorknob with his left hand and pushed the door open.

"Come on in," Barlowe invited.

He was depending on Percy to be his ace in the hole with his gun hidden by the desk, but as the woman entered with Clint Adams right behind her, Percy shouted something, stood up, and tried to shoot her. Barlowe was impressed as she smoothly shot Percy in the chest. The man fell back into his chair and died sitting there.

The fool had taken Barlowe's ace and tossed it out the window.

"What about you?" Clint asked Barlowe.

Barlowe shrugged.

"He was paying me, and he's dead. I'm willing to just walk right out of here and keep on going."

"It's not that simple," Anne Archer said. "You killed that woman in Lincoln."

"So? I was paid to do that by Percy. Blame him."

"The sheriff tried to frame me for your crime."

"He was also paid by Percy, and as you can see, he's dead. You have no reason to look for revenge against me, ma'am. I've done nothin' to you."

"What about Sheriff Macy?" Clint asked.

"What about him?"

"What did he do to you? You weren't paid to kill him. You can't expect me to blame Percy for that."

"He got in my way," Barlowe said. "It was his own fault."

"No," Clint said, shaking his head. "He had no chance against you and you knew it."

"Why was he there?" Barlowe asked. "Because you wouldn't face me yourself. How about taking the blame yourself?"

"I do," Clint said, pushing Anne Archer off to the side. "I blame myself and charge myself with making it right."

"And what's gonna make it right, Adams?" Barlowe asked.

"You and me, Barlowe." Clint holstered his gun as he issued the challenge. "Right now."

Barlowe stared into Clint Adams's eyes and suddenly knew he could not outdraw this man. He knew that if he touched his gun, Clint Adams would kill him.

"Hold on," Barlowe said. "There's a new sheriff in this town, you know. Why don't you just hand me over to him?"

"Why? So you can make him let you go? Not a chance."

"I—I'll confess," Barlowe said. "I'll tell him that I killed Sheriff Macy."

"What would that do, Barlowe?" Clint asked. "You'd hang, and that would cost the country money.

No, no, it's better this way."

Hank Barlowe was the first man Clint Adams had truly *wanted* to kill in a long time.

"Come on, Barlowe," he said. "You wanted this a few days ago. What's changed? Come on, let's do it."

Barlowe realized that Clint Adams was not going to let him off the hook and because of that he became angry.

"Goddamn you, Adams—" he said, and went for his gun.

Clint drew, easily besting the man, and fired three times. The first bullet struck Barlowe in the belly, causing him to drop his gun. He staggered but braced himself with a hand on the desk. Clint's second shot struck him in the chest, straightening him up. Before he could fall, though, Clint fired a third time, and this bullet pushed Barlowe back against the window, which shattered beneath his weight. The man went tumbling out the window. He was dead before he struck the ground, where he lay in the street with the other two men.

Anne looked at Clint and said, "That was personal and had nothing to do with me."

"It started with you," he said, ejecting the spent shells and replacing them with fresh ones, "but yeah, then it got personal—*more* personal."

FORTY-SEVEN

When Clint and Anne Archer returned to Lincoln, Nebraska, there was a federal marshal waiting there for them. Actually, he wasn't waiting for them. He was filling in for the deceased sheriff, while trying to find out who had killed the man.

On the way to Lincoln, Clint and Anne had come up with a story. They didn't know if it would work, because they had no one to really corroborate their story in Omaha, but they thought it was worth a try. It was better than Clint admitting he had killed Sheriff Chadwick. Once those words were out of his mouth, a federal marshal might not give him a chance to say any more.

They presented themselves at the sheriff's office and met Marshal Sam McGowan. McGowan recognized Clint's name and sat down behind the late Sheriff Chadwick's desk to listen to their story.

"So you're tellin' me that this man Barlowe killed the woman and then killed the sheriff, too?"

"That's right," Clint said.

"After trying to frame me for the first murder," Anne Archer said. "And I had just ridden into town that day and didn't know the woman."

"That's easy enough to check," the marshal said.

"Check it," Clint said. "And while you're at it, check on the killing of a Sheriff Macy over in Omaha."

"Barlowe did that, too?"

"That's right."

"And where's Barlowe now?"

"He's dead," Clint said. "He and the man he worked for, Michael Percy."

"And the dead woman was Percy's mistress?"

"Yes," Clint said. "You can check that with his widow."

"She knew about it?"

"Yes."

McGowan, a tall, rangy man in his forties who had been a lawman for over fifteen years, shook his head and said, "This is a lot to have to check up on, Mr. Adams, Miss Archer. You two, uh, are planning on staying in town until I get it all checked out, aren't you?"

"Of course, Marshal," Clint said. "We want this cleared up more than anyone."

They left the office and stopped outside.

"What do you think?" Anne asked.

Clint shrugged.

"If one of the witnesses who was in the saloon when Barlowe shot Macy speaks up, then we're okay. If not . . . we'll have to wait and see."

She looked at him and asked, "And what shall we do while we wait?"

They had already sent a telegram to her partners, Sandy Spillane and Katy Littlefeather, assuring them that she was all right, so there was only one thing Clint could think of.

If God came down from heaven and told Clint Adams that the world was going to end tomorrow and he had to get married today, Anne Archer would be the woman he picked.

Of course, he had never told her that.

All he ever told her was how beautiful she was, and now she was even more so. She had come a long way since they'd first met and there was nothing girlish about her anymore. She was all woman, and her body showed it.

He detected more heaviness in her breasts and hips, but it was not fat, it was maturity. As she sat astride him, he enjoyed her weight because it aided in burying him deeply inside of her. She rode him and he hefted her breasts, holding them in his palms, rubbing her nipples with his thumbs and then sitting up so he could kiss them and suck them while she rocked in his lap. He clasped her buttocks and pulled her to him, moaning as she cried out and then crying out as she bit him on the shoulder. Anne had always been an energetic lover and she was no less now. If anything, she was more eager, more anxious to please and be pleased, and in that he matched her.

Quickly, easily, he took hold of her, lifted her, and reversed their positions so that she was on her back. He crouched down between her legs and found her wet and salty and fragrant as he tasted her with his tongue working her into a blissful frenzy . . .

Later she did the same for him, licking him and sucking him lovingly, working on him until he was more swollen than ever before. When his release came, he thought he would die, but it felt so good he didn't care. . . .

They spent three days together in the hotel before Marshal McGowan notified them that everything they had said checked out.

"At least to my satisfaction," was the way he put it.

Apparently several of the people who were in the saloon the day Barlowe had killed Sheriff Macy came forward, and the rest just fell into place.

After they left McGowan, Anne asked Clint, "You don't think he's going to ask any more questions?"

"He's got a story he can live with now, Anne," Clint said. "He wants this to go away as much as anyone."

"I'm sorry I got you into this."

"Don't be," he said. "I don't like thinking about how it might have turned out if you hadn't asked me to meet you in Omaha."

They were in front of the livery, each holding the reins of their horses. She peered up at him, squinting her eyes against the sun, which was at his back.

"Want to come to California with me?" she asked. "The girls would love to see you."

"I've got to head back to Texas," he said. "The Southwest is calling me again. Give my love to Sandy and Katy."

They embraced and kissed, a kiss that went on forever and not long enough, and then they said good-bye.

For now.

Watch for

THE DENVER RIPPER

165th novel in the exciting GUNSMITH series
from Jove

Coming in September!

If you enjoyed this book, subscribe now and get...

TWO FREE

A $7.00 VALUE—

If you would like to read more of the very best, most exciting, adventurous, action-packed Westerns being published today, you'll want to subscribe to True Value's Western Home Subscription Service.

Each month the editors of True Value will select the 6 very best Westerns from America's leading publishers for special readers like you. You'll be able to preview these new titles as soon as they are published, *FREE* for ten days with no obligation!

TWO FREE BOOKS

When you subscribe, we'll send you your first month's shipment of the newest and best 6 Westerns for you to preview. With your first shipment, two of these books will be yours as our introductory gift to you absolutely *FREE* (a $7.00 value), regardless of what you decide to do. If you like them, as much as we think you will, keep all six books but pay for just 4 at the low subscriber rate of just $2.75 each. If you decide to return them, keep 2 of the titles as our gift. No obligation.

Special Subscriber Savings

When you become a True Value subscriber you'll save money several ways. First, all regular monthly selections will be billed at the low subscriber price of just $2.75 each. That's at least a savings of $4.50 each month below the publishers price. Second, there is never any shipping, handling or other hidden charges—*Free home delivery*. What's more there is no minimum number of books you must buy, you may return any selection for full credit and you can cancel your subscription at any time. A TRUE VALUE!

A special offer for people who enjoy reading the best Westerns published today.

WESTERNS!

NO OBLIGATION

Mail the coupon below

To start your subscription and receive 2 FREE WESTERNS, fill out the coupon below and mail it today. We'll send your first shipment which includes 2 FREE BOOKS as soon as we receive it.

Mail To: **True Value Home Subscription Services, Inc. P.O. Box 5235
120 Brighton Road, Clifton, New Jersey 07015-5235**

YES! I want to start reviewing the very best Westerns being published today. Send me my first shipment of 6 Westerns for me to preview FREE for 10 days. If I decide to keep them, I'll pay for just 4 of the books at the low subscriber price of $2.75 each; a total $11.00 (a $21.00 value). Then each month I'll receive the 6 newest and best Westerns to preview Free for 10 days. If I'm not satisfied I may return them within 10 days and owe nothing. Otherwise I'll be billed at the special low subscriber rate of $2.75 each; a total of $16.50 (at least a $21.00 value) and save $4.50 off the publishers price. There are never any shipping, handling or other hidden charges. I understand I am under no obligation to purchase any number of books and I can cancel my subscription at any time, no questions asked. In any case the 2 FREE books are mine to keep.

Name _____

Street Address _____ Apt. No. _____

City _____ State _____ Zip Code _____

Telephone _____

Signature _____
(if under 18 parent or guardian must sign)

Terms and prices subject to change. Orders subject to acceptance by True Value Home Subscription Services. Inc.

11688-2

J. R. ROBERTS

THE

GUNSMITH